A Christmas Tail

with the

Brooklyn Rink Rats

By

Barbara Williams

Chapter 1

This is a story about rats. But these aren't your ordinary rats. There's one thing that makes them special: They play hockey. Oh, and they can talk. I guess you can say that makes them a little special, too. But our story doesn't begin with the rats just yet. It begins with humans. Two boys, in fact, who are playing hockey.

"It's mine!" shouted Charles. He was short and lanky for an eight-year-old, but under the puffy winter coat he wore you could never tell. He scrambled down the street after the puck as his friend chased closely behind.

"Get back here!" Mike shouted.

They had been playing for the better of an hour and the score was tied. Because it was growing dark, they decided the next goal would win. And because both boys wanted to win, they desperately fought to see who would be the champion.

Charles put on a burst of speed, avoiding the icy patches in the street, and got control of the puck. He pushed it right and then left, drawing it closer to the tipped-over garbage can they were using as a goal.

Mike refused to give up. He dove forward and grabbed onto Charles's leg. Charles fell, crashing to the ground. Mike didn't hesitate. He climbed over Charles, stepping on his friend's back with his wet, smelly shoes.

"Hey, that's cheating!" Charles shouted.

Either Mike didn't hear or he didn't care. He ran over to the puck, pulled his stick back, and smacked it as hard as he could. The rubber disk sailed through the air and made a deafening crash as it slammed into the bottom of the garbage can.

Mike jumped up and down, raising his stick in triumph. "I won! I won!"

Charles slowly got up, brushing the dirt off his clothes. "That didn't count."

"What do you mean, 'That didn't count'?"

"Are you kidding me?" Charles yelled. "You cheated!"

"Did not!"

"Did so!"

The boys might have continued to argue if a loud rumbling hadn't broken the silence. A moment later, a large silver bus glided past, the words LONG ISLAND EAGLES emblazoned on the side in shiny red letters.

Mike's mouth dropped open. He had never seen a bus so big. "Whoa! Look at that!"

Charles stared. For a moment he, too, was speechless. Then he said, "Let's chase it! First one to touch it wins!"

That did it. The boys took off down the street.

The bus cut through town, weaving in and out of traffic. Eventually it pulled up to an old, dilapidated building.

What had once been new and prestigious fifty years ago was now old and worn-out. The brickwork was chipped and stained with graffiti, there were cracks in the concrete, and the acrylic light-up sign which read THE BROOKLYN ICE PALACE was faded and broken. Guarding the entrance were two large ceramic lions. At one point they had stood mean, proud, and ferocious. Now their teeth were chipped by the years of time, their long manes weathered away, making them look like overgrown cats.

"Got it!" Charles yelled.

"No, I got it!" shouted Mike.

They both slammed into the back of the bus, soot from their chase staining their faces.

The bus released a cloud of air pressure, like a dragon breathing out a puff of smoke. The door opened. A fat man wearing a dark blue suit two sizes too small stepped out. The fabric was stretched so tight that the buttons looked like they were ready to pop off. From his mouth dangled a big fat cigar that he lit, and on his head sat a baseball cap advertising Big Daddy's Sport Shop.

"Hey, you don't think that's Big Daddy, do you?" Mike asked.

Charles's eyes shot open. "It *is* him. My father told me about him."

"So did mine," said Mike. "He owns all those sport shops." He paused, marveling at the fact that he was so close to somebody so prestigious. "I think that's where my dad got my hockey stick."

"My father says he lives in a mansion on Long Island. I think he owns the Ice Palace, too."

"This dump? Why would he own a place like this?"

Charles shrugged. Before he could come up with a guess, Big Daddy shouted, "Let's go! Out of the bus! I'm not getting any younger!"

One by one, the Long Island Eagles made their way off the bus. There were a little over a dozen of them, fourteen to fifteen years old, each wearing brand-new matching warm-up outfits. They fell in line like a squadron of soldiers, lining up against the side of the bus.

Big Daddy pulled the cigar from his mouth, walking up and down the line, surveying his team. As he approached, each boy took a deep breath, stood up as straight as he could, and puffed out his chest.

"Good. But not good enough!" Big Daddy shouted. "I want you boys to be sharp. I want this to be a shutout, do you hear me? If those Brooklyn Rink Rangers get even one point on the board, one point, you're all doing push-ups! Got it?"

"Yes, sir!" the Eagles shouted back.

Big Daddy cocked his head, leaning in, looking disappointed. "What was that? I didn't hear you."

"Yes, sir!" the Eagles shouted again, this time even louder.

Big Daddy grinned, showing a gold tooth in his malicious smile. "Good. Then get in there and go kick some Ranger behind!"

It is at this point in our story that we must leave the two boys behind, possibly to quarrel over who touched the bus first, or possibly to get into whatever shenanigans boys their age get into. Instead, we must follow Big Daddy and his Eagles into the Brooklyn Ice Palace.

Chapter 2

The Brooklyn Rink Rangers' locker room looked just like the building: old, simple, and run-down. The paint on the walls were chipping and the benches wobbled. Somebody had even thrown balls of hockey tape into the hole of the light fixture on the ceiling. Nevertheless, the Brooklyn Rink Rangers were a good-natured, outgoing bunch. They might not have had the nice matching warm-up suits like the Eagles, but they had each other, and that's what counted.

They were the same age as the Eagles, and they had the same equipment, except theirs was older, torn, and slightly mismatched. Some of the numbers were faded, and some were of a different style altogether, as if they been bought at different times and ironed onto the jerseys.

The Rink Rangers didn't care. Each of them wore smiles on their faces.

Sitting off in the corner by his locker was a blond boy with big blue eyes. You couldn't tell because he was sitting and had a sad expression on his face, but he was tall for his age and had a great personality. In his hand he held a double-sided coin that he stared at.

He might have looked at it forever if a hand hadn't touched his shoulder.

"In my thirty years of running the Ice Palace, I've never seen someone so weary before a game," said an old man in his late sixties. He was thin and frail and wore a gray mustache that tickled his upper lip. "Are you okay?" Pops Anderson asked.

A.J. looked up. "The car accident happened a year ago today."

Pops frowned, wrinkles creasing the corners of his eyes. "I know . . . I miss your parents more than you can imagine."

He sat down next to A.J., the joints of his knees popping like firecrackers.

"My father gave this to me," A.J. said, holding out the double-sided coin. "He said that no matter what, I'd always be a winner."

The corners of Pops's lips turned up in a slight smile. "That *does* sound like your father. He was right, you know? You always will be a winner." He took A.J.'s hand and closed it into a fist around the coin. "You'll always make me proud."

"Thanks, Grandpa. I love you."

"I love you, too, A.J." A tear leaked out of Pops's eye, and he quickly turned his head to hide it.

A.J. hugged Pops. "It's almost game time. Don't worry, I'm gonna make you proud."

"You do that," said Pops. "You show those Eagles who's boss. And don't forget, have fun."

The Eagles were tough and ruthless, sticking to their defense and never letting up on offense. It would have been nice to say that the game was close, but that wouldn't have been true. In fact, the Brooklyn Rink Rangers wouldn't have scored at all if it hadn't been for A.J.—in the very last period he scored the one and only goal.

Even though he didn't show the Eagles who was boss, he still had fun.

At the time of the game, the arena had been loud and a flurry of activity. Now, an hour later, it was empty and quiet, except for Pops Anderson's office, where the old man sat in a chair with his face buried in his hands. There was a small light on his desk that illuminated the paperwork he had been going over.

Suddenly, there was a loud knocking on his office door. Before Pops even had a chance to say "Who is it?" Big Daddy pushed the door open and strode in, closing it behind him.

"Pops Anderson. Just the man I've been wanting to see."

"I hope you didn't come in to gloat," said Pops.

"Gloat? Now, why would I do that? My team doesn't deserve to gloat. They're still outside doing their push-ups. I'm here to talk about business."

Pops bit his lower lip, stealing a glance at the paperwork on his desk.

Big Daddy saw this. "I see we're on the same page. Well . . . ?"

Pops sighed. "I don't have it yet."

"What do you mean you don't have it yet? Your rent is five months past due."

"I know," said Pops. "I just don't have it. Times have been hard lately."

Big Daddy pulled a cigar out of his pocket, inspecting the wrapping. "Your rent is the only thing keeping me from demolishing this dump and building one of my sports shops. What's the point of me keeping it if you're not going to pay me my rent?"

"I'll get you your money," said Pops. "Can you give me an extension? Just six more months?"

Big Daddy laughed. "Are you kidding me? That's a joke, right? Just like your Rink Rangers are a joke."

"Please," Pops begged. "I'm asking you from my heart."

"Fine," said Big Daddy. "I'll give you an extension. And this is from my heart, too. I'll give you to Christmas."

Pops nearly fell off his chair. "That's one week! You can't be serious."

"I can, and I am. Christmas day and not one minute past."

"But what about the children? Where will they play? They need this place."

Big Daddy laughed, a big baritone sound that nearly shook the room. "The children? I don't care where the little monsters go as long as they buy my gear. And they'll have a chance to do that just as soon as I bulldoze this dump and build something a little more . . . *inviting*," he finished, looking at the cracked walls and dirty floor.

"You're the monster," said Pops.

Big Daddy looked at him, aghast. "Excuse me?"

"You heard me. All you care about is money. You're a horrible person."

Big daddy strode over to Pops's desk. He reached over and grabbed the old man's shirt, pulling him up out of his chair. "Don't you *ever* speak to me like that, do you hear me? *Ever!*"

At that moment the door burst open again. This time, instead of a man striding in, it was A.J. His face was twisted in a bout of rage. He shot his finger out, pointing at Big Daddy.

"Leave my grandfather alone!"

Taken by surprise, Big Daddy loosened his fingers. It was

enough to allow Pops to slip out of the big man's grip.

"Well, look who it is," Big Daddy said, taking a careful look at A.J. "You've got a lot of nerve coming in here after scoring on my Eagles like that."

A.J. pretended as if he hadn't heard him. "Leave my grandfather alone," he repeated.

"Look, your grandfather and I were just having a difference of opinion. This is grownup stuff. Why don't you go back to whatever it is you were doing and let us take care of it."

A.J. took a step forward. "I'm not leaving."

Big Daddy put the cigar back in his mouth. "Fine, kid, have it your way." He turned back to Pops. "Remember, you have till Christmas. No later." With that, he spun around and walked out the door, brushing past A.J. and nearly bumping him over in the process.

"What was that about?" A.J. asked.

Pops slumped down in his chair, shaking his head. "He's after the rent. He said if I can't pay him by Christmas he's going to tear the rink down and build a sports shop."

A.J. looked mortified. "He can't do that!"

Pops sighed. "Unfortunately, he can."

"What are we gonna do? How are we gonna get the money?"

"Don't worry," said Pops. "Everything's going to be all right." Although it looked as if he didn't really believe himself.

"How?" A.J. asked. "How is everything gonna be all right?"

Pops looked up towards the ceiling, and quite possibly through it, towards the sky and the stars beyond. "It's Christmas time. Miracles happen." Under his breath, he added, *I hope.*

A.J. came around the desk. "I don't like this, Grandpa."

"I'll take care of it. You just focus on playing hockey. By the way," he added, "your parents would have been proud of you for standing up to Big Daddy like that. I know I am."

A.J. looked at his grandfather with admiration. "Really?"

Pops put a reassuring hand on his shoulder. "Are you kidding me? Did you see the look on Big Daddy's face? It looked like he'd seen a ghost!"

A.J. smiled. "Thanks, Grandpa."

Pops smiled back. "Come on, it's getting late. Let's go home."

Together they shut off the lights and locked the doors. By now it was pitch black outside and the wind had picked up, forcing them to duck their heads into their coats as it nipped at their faces. Perhaps that's why they didn't see the hockey player walking towards them on the sidewalk. Or perhaps it was because the hockey player was only six inches tall . . .

Chapter 3

It's true that hockey players come in all shapes and sizes. To the humans, Guido Lombardi might have seemed tiny, but to his fellow rats, he was the tallest of the bunch. The thick snow jacket he wore to protect himself from the icy weather hid his athletic build. And the wool-knit hat with the Italian flag colors he wore over his head hid his pointy ears. As he walked, he leaned to one side to compensate for the large hockey bag slung over his shoulder. Inside was all his gear, including the jersey with the letter C stitched over his heart, indicating that he was the captain.

Guido ducked his head against the biting wind and walked on. He could have made it to the rink sooner if he'd finished his chores at his father's pizzeria. Although he knew that wouldn't have made any difference, since he had to wait for the humans to leave anyway. Now that they were gone, the rats would play.

In fact, the rats *had* been playing, as far back as he could remember. There was another whole world right below the humans' feet they didn't know about: a city with restaurants, shops, buildings, and fairs. The only thing missing was an ice rink, which was why Guido and his team had to endure the long hike up to the street to play at the human rink.

I must be crazy being out in this blizzard, he thought. He knew why he was doing it though. It was because his team was playing the Manhattan Maulers in two days. If they beat them, then they'd move on to the championships and play the Canadians, a team which had won the past four years. Guido and his team desperately wanted to beat the Canadians, which was why they needed to practice. But first they needed to find a new goalie.

Guido paused, making the sign of the cross as he thought about poor Marco (the world could be a dangerous place to a six-inch-tall rat).

In time, he made it to the Ice Palace. The big building stood dark and quiet, the wind howling in the night, sending shivers up Guido's spine. Pops Anderson and A.J. had locked the doors to the main entrance, but there was another entrance they didn't know about, this one on the side of the building too small for them to see. It was this entrance that all the rats used.

Guido was just about to reach for the handle on the little door when the wind howled again. The welcome sign above it banged ferociously against the building. A low rumbling filled the night. Guido looked up to see an avalanche of snow fall from the roof. He tried to scramble away but the large hockey bag weighed him down like an anchor. One second he was standing there, the next he was buried in over a foot of snow. The only part of him sticking out of the white fluff was his tail, resembling a submarine periscope with an icicle hanging off the tip.

Guido turned his tail first left, then right, then thrust his head out of the snow, gasping for air. "Great! Just great!" He clawed his way out of the pile, pulling his bag after him.

He stood back, surveying the cave-in blocking the entrance. There was no way he could move all that snow. How was he going to play hockey now?

Not knowing what else to do, he made his way to the back of the building. As he approached, he noticed light coming from a small crack in the foundation.

Looks like the team's already inside. He made his way over to the crack, hoping it wasn't too small for him to squeeze through. Out of nowhere, a scraggly paw came down, blocking his path.

It belonged to a huge gray and white alley cat. The beast looked like it hadn't taken a bath in weeks. Its fur was disheveled, its whiskers stiff as barbwire. Above them were a pair of piercing yellow eyes that nearly made him freeze in place. Below, a mouth filled with crooked, spiked teeth parted to let out a long runner of drool, oozing to the ground, smoking in the cold night.

Guido swallowed, hard. The puffy winter coat had been doing a good job to keep him warm. Now he shivered violently, all the color draining from his face.

"Ah, a late-night snack," said Sid the Alley Cat, surveying his dinner.

"Y-y-you . . ." stuttered Guido. It took him a moment to gather himself. "It's you. You ate Marco."

Sid grinned. "And he tasted divine. The only question is, will you taste better?" With that, he lunged at Guido. Guido lurched backwards, barely avoiding Sid's paw as it came down. He fell on his back, tumbling away. Sid wasted no time. The cat jumped again, this time batting Guido with his paw. Guido rolled on top of the snow and smashed into the building. His hat flew off somewhere during the scuffle.

He got up, shaking his head. The world was spinning. Through blurry eyes he could make out a shape coming towards him. He tried diving aside but was too slow. Sid's paw came down and trapped his tail.

"Now where's the fun in eating my dinner if I can't play with it first?" said Sid. As he talked, he brought his face down to Guido's level, his sour breath nearly choking the rat.

"Let me go!" Guido shouted.

To his surprise, Sid did. Then he felt himself rolling on top of the snow as Sid swatted him again. He came to rest a few feet away, staring at the sky. The clouds were gone and the stars were visible. Guido knew he'd need a miracle to survive. He kept looking at the sky, his body aching, hoping he'd see a shooting star to wish upon. Instead, he saw Sid's ugly face as the cat approached.

If Guido had been any other rat he might have given up. But Guido was not like any other rat. Guido had the letter C stitched on his jersey, and that made him important. He was the captain of his team. As a captain he had the duty to lead them through the championships. Giving up was not an option, especially now.

Guido rolled over. When Sid pounced, he dove aside.

The cat loosed a vociferous growl, clearly annoyed that his meal was trying to escape. Guido didn't pay it any attention. He just ducked his head and put on a burst of speed, running faster than he had ever run in his life, his little feet making tracks in the snow.

"Get back here!" Sid roared.

Guido didn't look back. He didn't need to. By the putrid breath steaming his ears, he already knew that Sid was hot on his trail. He didn't even pause to grab his hockey bag. He just stuck his paw out like a hook and grabbed the handle, pulling it behind him. The weight slowed him down, but the crack in the wall was only a foot away.

"Stop!" Sid cried.

Guido did no such thing. In fact, Guido jumped, diving forward, putting his paws out like a swimmer.

Sid dove as well. The alley cat soared through the air, chasing its dinner, its slavering mouth parting to accept the feast.

The front half of Guido's body slipped into the crack. The back half with the bag got stuck. Had there been more time he might have started to worry, but everything happened so fast that he didn't have a chance.

Sid slammed into the wall, trying to bite down on Guido's tail. The impact was so sudden that it pushed Guido and his hockey bag the rest of the way through the crack.

Inside the rink, Guido patted down his body, amazed that he had escaped. He was missing the hat Gia had made him, but that was a small price to pay for his life. When he was sure that he was still in one piece, he reached into the crack and pulled his hockey bag through. The sight behind it caused his heart to leap into his throat again: a pair of piercing yellow eyes glared at him from the other side of the crack.

"You got lucky," Sid growled. "But you won't be so lucky next time. I can promise you that."

Chapter 4

At night, the inside of the rink was eerie and foreboding. The long labyrinthine hallways twisted like a maze. The staircase descending to the basement locker rooms was dark and ominous. It led to a single door at the end of the hallway. The scene behind the door, however, was the complete opposite: bright and cheery. Guido pushed it open to a welcoming embrace by his team.

"What took you so long?" one of them asked.

"I thought the captain's supposed to be the first one here," joked another.

Guido told them all about his narrow escape, sparing no detail. As he did, everyone turned to the corner of the locker room, where a tiny Christmas tree decorated with lights—green, white, and red—and a silver angel stood above a picture frame. The inscription read *Marco, forever in our hearts.* Inside was a photograph of a plump rat in goalie equipment.

After his story, Guido made his way over to the tree. He peered at the angel, shedding its light, illuminating the locker room. Then he slowly lowered his gaze to the picture frame.

"You were an amazing goalie, Marco. And Sid is an evil, wretched thing. It's not fair that you're gone. I just hope we can find somebody as good as you before we play the Canadians."

Guido might have said more, but the sight of an unfamiliar box next to the tree robbed his attention. There was a red blanket in the box, and the blanket was *twitching . . .*

Curious, Guido reached in. When he pulled the blanket aside, he nearly had a heart attack.

"What is that thing?" he screeched, his pulse quickening.

Several of the rats came over to see what the commotion was all about.

A tiny black kitten peered up out of the box, its calm blue eyes nearly as big as its head.

Carmine Ponzini—also known as Cream Puff by his teammates—a husky rat with a big belly who wore a red vest with hundreds of pockets, said, "I found him out by the dumpster crying. He was so small I had to take him in. I named him Oscar."

Several of the other rats gasped.

"But he's a *cat!*" said Guido.

Cream Puff looked down, kicking at some dirt on the floor.

"I know, but he's only a baby. Maybe we could bring him up and, you know, teach him what's right and wrong."

"But he's still a cat! You can't teach him to go against nature. Get him out of here!"

"But it's so cold outside, and he's so little. Look at him."

Guido had to admit he did look cute. Also, he was still so small there was no way he would pose any danger to them. At least for now.

"I don't know. What do you guys think?" he asked, turning to the others.

A skinny, lanky rat wearing a button-down shirt with suspenders tucked into knickers, black horned-rimmed glasses, and a plaid golf cap said, "Well, I'm usually allergic to cat's, but this one doesn't seem to bother me. At least not until he's bigger."

"You're sure, Nerdy?"

Nerdy nodded. "It really is freezing outside. The poor little thing wouldn't last a day. Call it Karma, us taking him in." He walked over to the box, surveying the kitten inside. "Besides, we can study him for the time being. See what makes cats tick. Maybe learn new ways to escape them."

The other rats seemed to like this idea.

"Well?" Cream Puff pleaded.

"Okay, we can keep Oscar," Guido said reluctantly. "But only until he's big enough to take care of himself," he added quickly.

Cream Puff enveloped Guido in a huge hug. "Thank you, Captain! I promise he's gonna be the best mascot ever!"

Guido rolled his eyes. *A cat for a mascot. What's this world coming to?*

Cream Puff pulled a cream puff out of one of the many pockets on his vest. The rat held the tiny pastry out for Oscar, who first licked it shyly, then began to nibble on it. Several of the other rats laughed.

"Looks like he's got a taste for cream puffs. Better watch out, Cream Puff," one of them said.

Cream Puff paid them no attention, stroking Oscar's fur as the kitten nibbled away at the treat.

Guido turned to Nerdy. "Are the rest of the guys here?"

Nerdy nodded. "Yup. They're all on the ice. All but Coach Lucky. He's still running a bit late."

"Hopefully Sid's left by now and he'll be okay getting in. The front door's blocked by snow, and I had to squeeze through a crack around back."

"I wouldn't worry about Lucky," said Nerdy. "You know how resourceful he is."

"You're right. Time to get dressed and run those drills."

Nerdy, who was wearing tan slacks and a plaid shirt, pulled at his clothes, ripping them off like Superman, exposing his hockey gear beneath. Guido just stared at him in amazement.

"What?" Nerdy said. "It saves me exactly seven and a half minutes."

Guido just shook his head, laughing. "You never cease to amaze me. I'll meet you out there."

"Sounds good to me," said Nerdy. "Hey, Cream Puff, let's go!"

Cream Puff launched himself out of Oscar's bed. By now he was covered from head to toe in cream puff goo. He looked down at himself, noticing the mess, and used his big tongue to lick himself clean.

"I'll be back in a little while," he said, turning to Oscar.

The kitten purred, contentedly nibbling away at the cream puff crumbs Cream Puff had left behind.

Just like Nerdy had said, the rest of the rats were on the ice, a hodgepodge of short and tall players, thick and thin. One of them, the starting right wing named Marcello Rinaldi, was stick-handling the puck, practicing his skill. He was Italian but worked in a French restaurant as a waiter.

Guido, now out of the locker room, skated up to him and stole the puck, crossing over to gain speed down the ice. "Thanks for the puck, lover boy!" he playfully called back.

Marcello, a good skater as well, raced after him. "Oh la la," he said in a French accent, "those are some fancy moves, Mona Lisa."

Cream Puff chased after them but caught an edge and fell, sliding down the ice on his big belly. He didn't seem to mind. In fact, he pulled another cream puff from somewhere out of his jersey and popped it into his mouth as he slid.

Nerdy joined in the fun, too, tapping his stick on the ice. "Over here!" he shouted.

Guido passed the puck. Nerdy accepted it. Just before he could cross the blue line on the other side of the ice, Sergio De Giuseppe, their right defenseman, checked him into the boards. He was a tall rat, like Guido, but nearly twice as wide and built like a Mack truck with bulging muscles. "Not so fast, bookworm," he joked. "Shouldn't you be reading something?"

Nerdy slammed into the boards and staggered to stay on his feet. When he composed himself, he shook his head, clearing it. Then he pushed the horn-rimmed glasses, which had fallen down, back up on his nose. "I should have predicted that," he said.

Sergio wasted no time. He skated as fast as he could towards the goal at the other end of the rink. He might have made it, too, if the blade of a stick with three stripes of red tape on it hadn't slipped between his legs. It belonged to Angelo De Luca, the most talented stick-handler on the team.

"Step aside, Mack Truck, a Corvette is coming through," he

said, laughing. He tapped Sergio's left skate, then pulled his stick out from under Sergio's legs and brought it in front, lifting Sergio's stick off the ice and stealing the puck.

"Give that back!" Sergio shouted.

"Not on your life!" Angelo brought the puck down the ice, weaving in and out of players. When he saw Nerdy coming towards him, he stopped as hard as he could, the blades of his skates digging into the ice. They sheered off the top layer, spraying Nerdy, covering him entirely in slush.

Nerdy fixed his glasses again. "I should have predicted that, too," he mumbled to himself.

Angelo kicked the puck with his skate and took off again. Guido and Marcello chased after him. Even Cream Puff joined in the fun.

"You'll never score!" Guido shouted. "Not even with an open net!"

"My friend is right, Mon Cherri," yelled Marcello. "Your time is up."

Angelo could only smile. "Don't be too sure about that!"

He pulled back his stick and drove it forward. His slap shot was hard and fast, but precise and incredibly accurate, too. The puck cleaved through the air, sailing towards the net.

A deep popping sound echoed throughout the rink as a goalie mitt closed around the puck.

Everyone stopped.

Nerdy adjusted his glasses. One minute the net had been empty, the next there was a blur and the mitt was in front of it. "I would have never predicted *that,*" he said.

The mitt was being held by a rat they had never seen before. He had a strong build, an intimidating swagger, and bright red hair under the helmet he pulled off.

Standing next to him was a rat identical to his description. If one glanced too quickly, he might have thought he was seeing double.

"I hear your team is in need of a goalie," said the first rat in a deep Irish brogue.

"I'm far better than my brother Patrick any day of the week," said the second rat. "Pick me."

Patrick blew out a puff of air, pushing his brother's shoulder. "You wish." He turned to the other rats. "I can skate circles around Brian here."

Brian laughed. "Yeah, if circles were squares."

Guido gave Nerdy a confused look. "Do you know these two?"

Nerdy quickly pulled out a clipboard. He fiddled with a few papers and fixed his glasses.

"Umm . . . wait, yes, they're right here—the O'Shaunessay brothers from Bay Ridge. They're coming down tonight to try out."

"That's right," said Patrick in his Irish accent. "Although

we can just skip past the 'try out' part if you want."

"That's right," said Brian. "We're even better when we're warmed up."

Nerdy peered at his clipboard and pushed the glasses up on his nose again. "Hurmm . . . a Vinnie Monfredo is supposed to try out, too. Has anybody seen him?"

Patrick and Brian grinned as they imagined Vinnie banging on the inside of the locker they had stuffed him into.

"He's not gonna make it," said Patrick, trying not to laugh.

"Yeah," said Brian, "you can say he's in a tight spot."

Nerdy scratched his head. "Okay . . . ?" He looked back down at his clipboard. "It says here you guys played a game that once lasted an entire day and then started a bar fight that lasted three."

Patrick looked up toward the ceiling, stroking the red hairs on his chin. "Ah, I remember that."

"Good times," agreed Brian. He pulled out his teeth and then pushed them back in. "Lost my fronts in that one."

Nerdy pulled off his glasses, blew fog onto the lenses, polished them, and put them back on, unsure if he'd seen things right. "Uh . . . right. It also says here that you two are no longer allowed to play in Bay Ridge."

Patrick nodded. "Banned us, they did."

"So how's about we play here with you lads instead?" asked Brian.

Sergio stepped forward. "I like 'em!"

"Me, too," said Cream Puff.

"Oui-oui," agreed Marcello. "They're tough. We're gonna need tough if we're to beat the Canadians."

Patrick elbowed his brother. "Get that, a French rat."

Brian let out a bark of laugher. "That's a bit out of the ordinary, wouldn't ya say? Listen to his accent."

"Look who's talking," mumbled Marcello.

Nerdy flipped a few pages on his clipboard, going over the O'Shaunessay brothers' background. "They are quite good from what I can see about their stats. Haven't let a goal past in fifteen games."

"Would'a been a whole season," said Brian.

"Yeah," said Patrick. "If they hadn't banned us."

As the three were having this exchange, Angelo skated over to Guido. "I do like them. A little rough around the edges, but we can work on that."

"I agree," said Guido. "I think they're exactly what the team needs right now." He turned to the O'Shaunessay brothers. "Welcome aboard! You two are officially Rink Rats! All you have to do is meet with Coach Lucky."

"Where is Lucky anyway?" asked Angelo. "He should have been here by now."

Guido agreed. "That's not like him. I hope everything's okay." He remembered his encounter with Sid earlier in the night and prayed that Lucky didn't get himself into a mess he couldn't handle.

Chapter 5

The Brooklyn Bridge, a large brick suspension bridge for both cars and foot traffic, provided shelter for all walks of life. On gloomy fall nights, men and women hard on their luck sought shelter from the pelting rain. On hot summer days, animals were drawn to its shadows to escape the scorching sun. And on spring evenings, just before twilight, many came to rest and take in the magnificent plant life that decorated the underside with diverse beauty.

However, deep in the corner, in the thicket of a thorn bush, lived a dark presence, a rat as evil as Sid the Alley Cat. His eyes were as red as fire, his hair spiked up like jagged spears. It came as no surprise that a rat as deceitful and wicked as him would choose a thorn bush for his hideout.

Spike ran a scarred paw through his spiked hair. "What do you say?" He looked down at the cards he held.

Sitting across the table from him was a thin rat dressed in a pin-striped suit. The fedora on his head and the gold chain around his neck complimented his outfit. He, too, held a set of cards.

Lucky bit his lip, starting at them. At last, he said, "I'm in." He pushed a few bills forward, adding to the pile in the center. There were only a few more bills on his side of the table, as if he hadn't been having the best of luck. On Spike's side rested a mountain of money, piled so high that it nearly covered his glaring red eyes.

The muscular rats surrounding the table—each one more muscular than the last—looked from their boss, to Lucky, and back again.

Spike's lips curled back into a sneer. "Feeling confident, are you? You must be feeling pretty . . . Lucky."

Lucky glanced down at his cards and bit his lip again. "Just show your cards, Spike."

"Gladly." Spike flipped them over, one by one.

As each showed its face, Lucky's heart dropped. He'd used the money for his sick mother's rent to play.

When all the cards were turned over, Spike gave Lucky a nod. "Your turn."

Lucky paled considerably.

When he didn't move, Spike repeated himself.

Lucky reluctantly flipped his cards over. As he did, Spike licked his lips with a diseased-looking tongue. "Three jacks," he said. "Normally that would be a fantastic hand. That is, if I didn't have these three kings." The smile that creased his face was as malevolent as ever. He reached forward, pulling the pile of money towards him. "Better luck next time."

"Spike, please," Lucky begged, "I need that money for my mother. She's sick, she—"

"Then you shouldn't have bet it," said Spike, simple as ever.

"Yeah, I know, don't risk what you can't afford to lose. My mother's been telling me that for years. This is different. I need twice as much than what I came here with by the end of the month or we lose the apartment. I had no other choice. Please, you've got to help me. I'll do anything."

The corners of Spike's lips curled up again, exposing his crooked teeth. "*Anything?*"

Lucky nodded. "Anything."

Spike rubbed his scarred paws together. "You have a big game coming up, I believe. If you beat the Manhattan Maulers, that is."

"Right," said Lucky. "Against the Canadians. It's the championship game."

"Tell you what, I'll give you a chance to make your money back, providing you make me a deal."

"What's the deal?"

"If you make it to the championships, you throw the game."

Lucky had to make sure he was hearing things right. "You mean you want me to betray my team and make them lose?"

Spike nodded. "And here I didn't think you were that smart of a rat." Spike's henchmen laughed. "I want you to throw the game. Final score: Canadians 4, Rink Rats 1. I'll even double your money if you do it. All of this"—he gestured to the pile on his side of the table—"when you beat the Maulers, the other half after you lose to the Canadians. Got it?"

Lucky got it, all right. He just didn't like it. "I don't know if I can do that to my team. They're like my family. They look up to me."

Spike waved a dismissive paw. "Suit yourself. The offer is on the table." He glanced at the table and laughed again. "Actually, your *money* is on the table. That, and a whole lot more. Tell you what: I'll give you until the night of the game against the Maulers to think about it."

Lucky sat in silent thought. Spike was offering him a lot of money. On the other hand, he'd have to betray his friends in order to get it. He knew it wasn't worth it, but then again he and his sick mother would be thrown out on the street if he didn't do it.

Spike didn't give him time to contemplate his decision further. He turned to his henchmen, who were cracking their knuckles and flexing their muscles, and said, "Gentlemen, if you would be so kind as to show this rat out. He's, how should I put it, *overstayed* his welcome."

Lucky began to get up on his own but Spike's henchmen

grabbed him by his arms, dragging him out, scuffing his shoes and soiling the cuffs of his pants along the way.

Chapter 6

Playing hockey at midnight is a curious thing. Normally, during that time, the body gets tired, you begin to yawn, and your eyes start to shut. Yet, when you're forced to play hockey so late because of the humans, you find that you're wide awake. Maybe it's the adrenaline pumping through your veins, or maybe it's because you're having so much fun, or maybe, it's the only time of the week when you can be surrounded by your best friends. Whatever the case, the Brooklyn Rink Rats practiced till all hours of the night.

That's why it came as no surprise when Guido looked up at the clock and saw that it was two in the morning.

"Oh no!" he cried. He pulled a whistle out of his pocket and blew it as loud as he could. "Practice is over! We ran late tonight! Hurry, we gotta go catch our subway!"

The rats scurried into the locker room, elbowing and bumping into each other along the way. There, they undressed with uncanny speed, not wanting to be stuck at the Ice Palace for the remainder of the night.

By now the biting wind outside had blown away the snow that had fallen in front of the entrance. Guido pushed the door open, stepping out into the blistering cold. "How are you guys getting home?" he asked the O'Shaunessay brothers.

"Don't worry about us, lad," said Patrick.

"Yeah," said Brian. "The O'Shaunessays take care of themselves."

With that, they hopped onto an old news truck passing by.

"Right on time!" Patrick said.

Brian waved to the others. "See you gents tomorrow!"

The mad dash to the subway proved an adventure of its own. The Rink Rats had to sprint down the sidewalk, carefully zigzagging around drifts of snow and avoiding the frozen patches in between. Twice, Cream Puff tripped and spilled some of his tasty treats onto the ground.

"Hurry up!" Angelo had yelled, helping him to his feet. "I refuse to get stuck out here in this weather!"

Thankfully they made it with time to spare.

"That was close," said Sergio, wiping a bead of sweat from his brow.

The subway station was blessedly warmer than it had been above ground. The rats were finally able to breathe without the chilled air stinging their throats. It was a lot brighter, too. Several lights hanging from the ceiling shed their brilliance to chase away the shadows. Slabs of concrete made up the floor, and faded mustard-yellow tiles decorated the walls. Not the best choice for interior design, but it suited the subway station just fine. Despite the presence of waste baskets, trash littered the platform, especially down in the gully with the tracks, just beyond the yellow caution strip marked with the words WATCH THE GAP.

It was here that the rats waited for the subway to arrive. They had taken the little staircase through the hole in the wall to descend to this level. There were maybe two or three other rats waiting around, bundled up in their winter coats, checking their watches. One of them had his face buried in a newspaper.

Guido was just about to check *his* watch when the ground began to vibrate and a light shone out of the end of the tunnel to his right. Like a groundhog emerging out of its burrow, the subway car escaped the tunnel, pulling into the station, its brakes squealing.

"Here's our ride, boys," Guido said to the others.

They entered through the trap door under the car the same time the humans above used the regular doors to step on. Once everyone was aboard, the doors above closed, the rats heaved the trap door shut, and the subway labored to life, lumbering out of the station and into the next tunnel.

Snuggly nuzzled into one corner of the compartment below the main car, Guido looked over each of his players. They all looked so tired. Many of them had their heads resting against the wall, their eyes closed. The ones who didn't were slowly nodding off, letting the gentle rocking of the car put them to sleep. He couldn't help but think that even though they were a team, each player had his own unique story.

Like Marcello, for instance. He worked in a French restaurant as a waiter and studied French a few nights a week at a local college. His ultimate goal was to one day open a French restaurant of his own, where he could entertain the ladies with his French accent. He could be described as suave and debonair. Nobody knew how, but he had his own fan club, where a bunch of girls came to the games, cheering him on. That was how he'd gotten the nickname *Lover-boy* from his teammates. They teased him about it, but they were secretly a little jealous, too.

Fast asleep next to him, snoring loudly, was Cream Puff. He still lived with his mother on Mott Street in Little Rataly. She owned a famous bakery in which Cream Puff helped out. Well, *helped out* wasn't the right term. If anything, he was the official taste tester, because he ate a lot of what she made. His deepest ambition, besides playing defense for the Rink Rats, was to one day own his mother's bakery. His mother was fine with this as long as he played hockey. She was glad he was on a team, making friends. Plus, she thought it would help him lose weight.

Nodding off across from Cream Puff was Nerdy. His real name was Rocco Bivona, but because he worked in the library and always had his head in a book, everyone called him Nerdy. He might have had his parents to thank for that. They both worked as professors at a college. Aside from playing hockey, he loved to write stories. In fact, he hoped to become a famous author one day.

Angelo's story was a bit darker than the others'. His parents had died in a car crash when he was eight years old. It was winter, like now, and a truck slammed into his parents' car while the three of them were driving to visit his grandmother. Angelo didn't remember much about the accident, only the paramedics cutting him out of the car and taking him away. Now Angelo lived with his grandmother, taking care of her. Guido wasn't surprised to find that Angelo was jerking his head every now and then, as if he were dreaming. By the way Angelo gritted his teeth, Guido had a feeling it was a nightmare. It seemed that this time of the year Angelo's dreams were always filled with nightmares. Every dream except his life goal, which was to play in the Rat NHL.

Lastly, Guido let his eyes roam over Sergio, who was staring out the little windows of the subway into darkness. He worked for his father's construction company, carrying metal beams, sheet rock, and lumber all day. It's what made him so strong. His father wanted him to take over the company when he retired, but Sergio wanted to become a policeman instead.

Having looked over his whole team, Guido closed his eyes, preparing to rest a little before his stop. As he did, he couldn't help but think of his own story. He worked at his father's pizzeria in Little Rataly, helping out the family and trying to make ends meet. But it wasn't the pizzeria in particular that he was thinking about. No, it was a certain female rat that worked there named Gia. Gia was the one who had knitted him the green, white, and red hat he had lost when Sid chased him. She had long blond hair, light blue eyes, and a beautiful smile. Guido's father hired her to be the cashier about a month ago. It was safe to say that Guido had a *huge* crush on her. The only thing was, he didn't know if she felt the same way about him.

Very slowly, he let his thoughts drift in her direction, slipping into a dream where he got up the courage to ask her out on a date.

Before he knew it, the subway car came to a halt, and he jerked awake. He blinked a few times and rubbed his eyes.

"Come on, guys!" he said. "Time to go home."

One by one, the rats woke up, making their way off the subway car.

Cream Puff yawned and dug his paw into his jacket, pulling out a half-eaten cream puff.

"Hurry up, Cream Puff!" Guido called from the platform.

Cream Puff popped the tasty pastry into his mouth and made his way through the trap door, shutting it behind.

Unfortunately this wasn't the end of their journey. Together, they made their way down the platform and over to a hole in the foundation. One at a time, they scurried in. Last but not least, Cream Puff waddled his way over. He sized up the hole like he always did and squeezed his way into it. Except, something different happened this time. Instead of barely making it through, he got stuck.

"Hey!" he called out to his teammates. "Wait up! I'm stuck!"

He struggled, bucking back and forth. When nobody came to his rescue, he began to panic.

"Guys? Can anyone hear me?"

He received only his echo in answer. Panicked that he may be stuck in the hole until morning, he tried jerking free again. Suddenly, he felt a rumbling in his stomach and let out a huge burp. If his cries had been loud, this was even louder. Thankfully the burp let out just enough air that he could slip through the hole.

In a minute he caught up to the rest of his teammates. Together, they embarked down the path over plumbing pipes, leaky valves, and broken concrete. Down and down they went, faster and faster, never missing a beat. Finally, they reached the ground.

"Ah, it's good to be home," said Sergio, taking in his surroundings.

Little Rataly stood dark and quiet in all of its magnificence. The outline of the city seemed to almost hover in the air, each building standing taller than the last.

It was here that the rats began to go their separate ways.

"'Till tomorrow," Marcello said, running into the night. "Au Revoir!"

Sergio tipped everyone a nod. "Got a busy morning, myself. "Goodnight."

"See you," said Angelo. He, too, made his way down the street and into the darkness.

Nerdy was about to follow suit when he realized that Guido didn't look like he was moving. "Everything okay?" he asked.

Guido looked around in surprise. "Huh? Oh, yeah, I'm fine. Just thinking."

"About what?"

Guido ran a paw through his hair. "Nothing really."

Nerdy eyed him suspiciously. "You're thinking an awful long time about nothing."

Nerdy did have a point. If it was nothing then why did he keep thinking about it? After a moment, he decided it couldn't hurt to confess.

"It's about Lucky . . ."

Nerdy nodded, seeming to understand. "You're thinking

about going over to his apartment to see why he wasn't at practice, aren't you?"

Guido didn't even have to answer. His silence was enough.

"I thought so," said Nerdy. "Be careful. I'd go with you, but I promised my parents I'd open the library tomorrow."

"Thanks," said Guido. "I appreciate it."

"Don't mention it." Nerdy took one last look back at his teammate then made his way off into the night. Guido watched him go, slowly vanishing into the darkness.

Chapter 7

If there was a word to describe Lucky's bedroom, it wouldn't be *extravagant*. In fact, it wouldn't be anything to describe greatness at all. It would be something more along the lines of *quaint* or *sparse*.

Lucky lived in a small apartment with an even smaller bedroom. All he had in it was his dresser and a bed. It was this last that he found himself in, sound asleep, the covers pulled up to his nose. He snored loudly, deep in a dream where he gambled over a hand of poker.

A small window stood above his bed. Had Lucky been a little better with money, he might have been able to afford blinds. As it was, the window was bare, the panes of glass allowing those outside a chance to look in.

It just so happened that somebody was looking in right now.

Guido stood on the dumpster outside Lucky's window, peering in. It hadn't taken him long to get there, and he was glad to find Lucky inside.

Not knowing what else to do, he tapped on the window.

"Hey, Lucky . . ."

Lucky snorted loudly and turned over.

Guido tapped harder. "Hey, Coach! Lucky . . ."

Lucky rolled over again, groggily parting his eyes. "Huh? What? Who—who's there?" He rolled over some more and fell out of bed. There was a loud *Thump!* as he crashed to the floor. He sprang to his feet a moment later with a baseball bat clutched tightly in his paws, his head jerking back and forth, his eyes frantically searching the room for the disturbance.

"Over here," Guido said, feeling a bit guilty. "At the window. It's me, Guido."

Lucky slowly put the bat down, squinting at the window. "Guido? What are you doing here so late?"

"I wanted to read you a bedtime story."

Lucky stared at him, a mixture of confusion and hate composing his expression.

Guido said, "I wanted to talk to you, okay? You weren't at practice. I wanted to make sure everything was all right."

"We had practice tonight?"

"Come on, Lucky, you know we did."

"I thought that wasn't until tomorrow." When Lucky saw the way Guido was glaring at him, he put his right paw over his heart and raised his left and added: "Honestly."

Guido gave him a cold, hard stare. "I don't believe you."

Lucky hung his head. "Fine, I'm sorry."

"That you just lied to me or that you weren't there?"

It took him a moment to answer. "Both, I guess."

Guido considered this. "Okay. I'll forgive you if you tell me why you didn't show up."

"Things kind of got out of hand. By the time everything was taken care of it was too late."

"What do you mean *things kind of got out of hand*? You know we play the Maulers in a few days. If we beat them then we get to play the Canadians. The team's counting on you."

Lucky sighed. "I know."

"Then why didn't you come?"

It took him a moment, but Lucky walked over to the window and pulled it open. "It's hard to explain."

"Try me," said Guido.

Lucky did, but he suddenly found it difficult to form words. In the end, he settled on, "Things just got out of hand. It won't happen again. I promise."

Guido nodded, not particularly satisfied, but knowing that was the best he was going to get. "Will you be at practice tomorrow?"

"Yes."

"Do you promise?"

"I promise."

"Okay. I'm holding you to that."

Guido started to turn around, preparing to jump off the

dumpster.

"Hey, Guido?"

Guido paused. "Yeah?"

"Thank you for caring."

"Why wouldn't I care?"

Lucky looked down at his paws as his knotted his fingers together, then about the room. He pretty much looked everywhere but at Guido. "Because a lot of rats would have given up on me by now."

"Not me," said Guido. "You're a Rink Rat, and we stick together. I'll see you tomorrow."

"I know," said Lucky. "Thanks. That honestly means a lot to me."

The rats said their goodbyes and Guido jumped off the dumpster, finally heading home for some much needed rest.

Chapter 8

The next morning arrived bright and sunny. Although in winter, bright didn't necessarily mean it was warm enough to melt the snow. People everywhere around town were still out shoveling. There was even somebody outside the Ice Palace shoveling the sidewalk. If one looked closely, he could see that it was Pops Anderson.

Pops had on a long brown coat, boots, mittens, and a floppy hat that covered his ears. It was just enough to keep him toasty as he did his work. It had taken him an hour, but he had shoveled most of the sidewalk from the front of the building to the back. He was just about finishing up when he found a bunch of animal tracks in the snow.

He bent down, his knees popping like always. He winced a little but ignored the pain as he inspected the prints. To him they looked like a cat's paw prints. And, wait, maybe a rat's, too? They were so sporadically placed that there could only be one meaning behind it: a struggle.

"Poor little guy," Pops said, standing up. He wondered if

the rat had gotten away or if the cat had found itself a snack.

Not particularly wanting to find out the answer, he got back to work. He picked up his shovel, thrust it into the snow, and stopped.

"What's this?"

Right below the blade rested a little green, white, and red hat, so little that he could fit it on the top of his thumb. Pops held it in the palm of his hand, inspecting it. He might have studied it more, but A.J. popped his head out of the doorway, interrupting him.

"Hey, Grandpa, everything's clean. I emptied all the trash bags and mopped the bathroom. Do you need any help shoveling?"

When Pops didn't answer, A.J. asked, "Grandpa? What are you looking at?"

Pops smiled, "Come take a look at this."

"What's that?" A.J. asked when he had come over.

"Tell me, what does this look like to you?"

A.J. stared at the tri-colored piece of fabric in his grandfather's hand. At first it looked like it had been one piece, but now that he looked closer, he could see that it was stitched together, as if somebody had taken the time to make it.

"I don't know," he said at last. "Do you?"

Pops thought he did. "I think it's a hat."

A.J. looked at him, confused. "A hat? But it's way too small for a hat."

Pops pointed out the tracks on the ground. "It seems that we're not the only ones who have a home here at the Ice Palace, after all."

Chapter 9

One might have expected Little Rataly, the underground city of the rats, to be dark, dreary, and desolate because of its location. Dampness, shadows, and mold usually comes to mind with places like that. Little Rataly was nothing of the sort. It was true that it was underground, but there were so many storm grates in the city above that the city below was bathed in sunlight. At noon, not even a shadow could hide.

It was a real city, too. There were tall buildings, short buildings, buildings under construction. Rats in suits hustled their way down the sidewalks and across parking garages to get to work. Some carried briefcases, others backpacks. There were street vendors, performance artists, cab drivers, and rats selling tickets to Broadway shows. Police rats directed traffic while fire rats put out fires. Teacher rats taught while little rats played in the school yard. There were mail rats in white uniforms, delivering mail, and news rats tossing stacks of newspapers off the backs of news trucks.

If one looked closely he might see Sergio at one of the

construction sites, curling heavy paint cans as he walked, or Angelo standing outside a skate shop with numerous pairs of skates hanging over his shoulder, waiting for the skate sharpener to open his doors for the day. One might even catch a glimpse of Nerdy at the library or Marcello at his French restaurant, wiping down the front window and turning the CLOSED sign to OPEN.

Certainly one would see Guido at his father's pizzeria. Its contemporary Italian décor made it hard to miss. It was a small shop but very cozy and stylish. It was the type of place you might walk into and feel right at home.

Behind the counter, working the register, was a short, tan rat. She had long blond hair, bright blue eyes, and a beautiful smile. She wore a green apron and had her hair pulled back into a ponytail. She moved around quickly, as if her duties would never end, cleaning dishes, wiping down the counter, all the while tending to the cash register. Yet, even though she was busy, she still made the time to say hello to Guido as he came out of the back with a bunch of pizza boxes in his arms.

"Good morning, Guido."

Guido nearly tripped and spilled the boxes. He blushed, his cheeks turning a deep shade of crimson.

"'Morning, Gia. How's your day so far?"

"Pretty good. A little busy. How about yourself?"

Guido looked at the pizza boxes that had almost fallen to

the floor. Then he looked at Gia and at the beautiful smile she wore on her face. He was about to say *It's better now,* when he realized he wasn't wearing the hat she had made for him. "Uh, it's fine," he said quickly and hustled into the back.

Gia gave him a puzzled look. Wondering if she had done something wrong, she followed him. "Is everything okay?"

"Sure, everything's fine," said Guido, keeping his back to her as he busied himself with a mop. "Just want to get this place cleaned up before my parents get here, you know how it is."

Gia didn't think that was it one bit. "No, it actually seems like you're trying to avoid me. Did I do something wrong?"

The idea was devastating. Guido couldn't let her think that. "No!" he nearly shouted. Then calmer: "No, not at all. It's just . . ."

He might have gotten it out, but his parents walked in, stealing the spotlight.

"Good morning, everyone," said Big Tony in his baritone voice. "Another beautiful day we're having in Little Rataly, aren't we?" He turned to Guido. "Thanks for opening up the shop." Then he looked over to Gia. "You, too. I appreciate the both of you being here so early."

Tony straightened the fedora on his head. He was a big rat, almost six inches tall, and nearly just as round with a thick handlebar mustache that wiggled back and forth when he talked. He wore a gray vest that was splitting at the seams and a white collared shirt beneath. Around his neck hung a gold chain with a St. Christopher's medallion on it.

"Yes," said his wife Maria. "We needed to take care of some things at the bank." She glanced at the empty pizza boxes Guido had brought in from behind. "Now that that's done, we can get to work and make some pizzas!"

She was a corpulent woman herself, matching her husband, although not nearly as round. If one looked at Guido's parents, they would have never guessed that Guido came from them, being so in shape. Perhaps it was owning a pizzeria and years of eating pizza and pastries that did it for his parents. Yet, that didn't change how nice they were. Tony was the most generous rat anyone had ever met, donating money to the orphanage every Christmas. Maria followed closely behind, cooking pastries for the PTA and church. Sometimes, if she saw somebody come into the store with little rats, she'd even give them a free desert, just because.

It wasn't very hard to miss her doing this. Not because of her size, or because of her boisterous attitude, but because of the bright blond hair on her head. She sometimes let it down if she was in a hurry, but she usually teased it up into a big bee's nest.

"Great idea," said Tony. He wrapped his arm around his wife—or as much as he could get it around her—pulled her in, and gave her a kiss on the cheek.

Gia giggled. "You two are so cute together."

Guido clearly didn't agree. "Gross!" he said, and quickly disappeared into the back.

"What's with him?" asked Maria.

Gia waved a dismissive paw in his direction. "Who knows. He's been like that all morning."

Tony shrugged, then rubbed his paws together. "Who's in for making pizzas?"

"You know I am," said Maria.

"I'll be right with you guys," said Gia. She wove her way into the back of the shop, where she found Guido busying himself with a mop. "What's up with you today?"

Guido quickly turned away when he saw her. "What do you mean?"

"That!" said Gia. "Right there! You turned away from me!"

"No, I didn't."

"Are you kidding me?" She reached out and spun him around so he faced her. "You're really trying to tell me you didn't just turn away from me when I started talking to you?"

It took Guido a moment for it to sink in that she had just grabbed his shoulders. When he did, he blushed again. Gia seemed to realize the same thing, because she let go and began to blush, too.

"Okay," he said at last. "I guess I am kind of avoiding you."

The color in Gia's cheeks immediately vanished. What replaced it was a deep sense of fear that he didn't like her. She tried to say something, but her throat suddenly felt very dry. Finally, she managed, "Y-you are?"

Guido nodded. He hung his head, refusing to look at her. "Yeah, but only because I lost the lucky hat you made for me. I didn't want you to be mad."

The dryness in Gia's throat vanished, as if Guido's words were an oasis she had drank from. "Oh! Is that all? That's okay."

Guido raised his head. "Wait, you're not mad?"

Considering the alternative, Gia was not mad at all. "It's only a hat," she said, trying to disguise her relief.

"Yeah . . ." said Guido, "but it's my *lucky* hat. You made it for me. I need it for the game against the Canadians." *And I need it for when I finally get up the courage to ask you on a date,* he wanted to add.

"Where did you lose it?" Gia asked.

"At the Ice Palace."

"Then let's go find it."

Guido considered this. "It may be too dark by the time we get out."

"So let's go now."

"Now?"

"Sure, why not?"

Guido could probably come up with a dozen reasons, but he chose the most logical one to say. "Because, my father will never let us leave. Our shifts just started."

Gia pulled a compact out of her purse. "Leave your father to me." She pushed her lower lip out, squeezed her eyebrows together, and tilted her head, putting on a sad puppy-dog face. She studied it in the mirror. When it was to her liking, she entered the front of the store, where Tony and Maria were kneading dough. "Excuse me, Mr. and Mrs. Lombardi . . ."

Tony and his wife paused. "Yes?"

"Do you mind if I step out for a little while with Guido? We'll be back soon, I promise."

Tony looked at the clock. "Where on earth would you be going? We'll have customers in a few hours. There are no pizzas in the oven!"

"Just for a walk. Something *is* bothering Guido, and he wants to talk about it. I figured there's no point in him working if he's only going to put in half the effort, you know?"

Tony seemed to think that half the effort was better than no help at all. "But the pizzas . . ."

Maria put a paw on her husband's shoulder. "Go, my dear. Find out what's bothering him and snap him out of it. We'll be here when you get back. We can definitely use one hundred percent effort from the both of you."

Gia beamed. "Thank you, Mrs. Lombardi. You, too, Mr. Lombardi." She nearly tripped in her hurry to the back room.

"Well?" Guido asked when she returned.

"We can leave, but we need to be back in an hour, two hours max."

Guido looked shocked. "Wow, I can't believe you got my dad to agree to that."

"It was actually your mom. Thank her. Come on, let's go. We don't have too much time."

They exited through the back of the pizzeria and hurried out onto the sidewalk.

"What's the subway schedule?" Gia asked.

Guido shrugged. "I only know the night schedule. I've never been to the rink in the daytime."

"Really?"

"Well, yeah, all the humans are there during the day." He paused for a second. "Wait a minute. I know someone who can help us."

"Who?"

"Nerdy."

Chapter 10

Nerdy stood on tiptoe on a rickety wooden ladder. It wobbled dangerously back and forth like it was in an earthquake. If he hadn't had a tail to use for balance, he might have fallen over. He reached up as high as he could and placed a book in an empty space between two novels on the top shelf.

"Here you go. Right back home."

He had several more books clutched to his chest. Nerdy surveyed the remainder of the library shelf. When he realized that the books belonged across the room, he climbed down the ladder.

"Hey, Nerdy."

Nerdy jumped, the books scattering across the floor.

"Don't do that!" he cried, turning around. "What if I was still up on the ladder and I— Oh, hey, Guido. Hey, Gia. What are you guys doing here?"

Gia bent down and helped him pick up the books. "We need your help. We don't know the subway schedule."

"Is that all? Where are you guys going?"

"To the rink," said Guido. "I dropped my lucky hat on the sidewalk outside."

"That's no problem at all," said Nerdy. "You can take the R if you walk down to—"

Before he could finish his sentence, Gia grabbed his paw, pulling him out of the library. "Excellent! Show us!"

Just like Nerdy had said, getting to the Ice Palace wasn't a problem at all—the R took them the whole way. During the ride, Guido told Gia about his encounter with Sid the Alley Cat, and how he had barely escaped with his life. Gia had gasped, reassuring Guido more than ever that it was okay he had dropped the hat. She scooted closer so they were barely an inch apart and stared him deep in the eye and told him that some things were more important than clothes. Guido could smell the perfume on her skin. He gulped, feeling his heart thud against his chest. Had he and Gia been alone, he might have summoned up all of his courage and used this opportunity to grab her paw and tell her how he felt, but Nerdy was sitting directly across from them, and he was too embarrassed.

Now the three of them stood on the sidewalk, the Ice Palace looming behind like a dilapidated mausoleum.

"Is this where it happened?" Gia asked.

Guido nodded. They were standing in the exact spot he had encountered Sid that night. "This is the spot, only . . ."

"The sidewalk wasn't shoveled at the time, was it?" Nerdy asked.

"No," Guido agreed, "it wasn't."

Gia looked at the two of them, trying to decipher the conversation. "Wait, so what's that mean?"

Guido gestured towards the big pile of snow to their left. "It means my hat's probably buried in that mountain of snow right there. Somebody must have come along and shoveled since the last time we were here."

If Gia had been a negative rat, she might have sulked at the idea of Guido's hat being buried and lost forever, but Gia always looked to the positive side of things. "What if somebody picked it up and brought it inside?"

"Who would have done that?" Guido asked. "It's so small."

"You never know," was Gia's response. "Stranger things have happened."

"She's right," said Nerdy. "Quantum mechanics states that the hat is simultaneously buried in the snow and safe inside the rink. Quantum supposition can only end when one finds the hat and reality collapses into one possibility or the other."

Guido and Gia just stared at him with looks of confusion stamped on their faces.

Nerdy sighed. "It means that if there's a possibility of the hat being in both places, I'd rather find it in the rink than having to dig through that mountain of snow."

"So we should look in the rink?" Guido asked.

"Yes," said Nerdy. "We should look in the rink."

Chapter 11

Pops Anderson sat behind his desk in his office at the Brooklyn Ice Palace. He had the phone pressed against his ear, in the middle of a heated conversation.

" . . . but you know I don't have that kind of money."

Pops pressed his hand against his forehead, looking distraught.

" . . . I already tried, believe me. The bank won't give me another loan."

He pulled the phone from his ear, turning it away from his head as a gruff voice shouted on the other end. When it subsided, he put it back.

In a moment, he added, ". . . but it's their home! They'll have nowhere else to play! They need this place more than I do. I'm doing it for them."

Pops surveyed his desk, needing to busy himself with something before the conversation drove him insane. He settled on the tiny hat he had put on top of his computer monitor. He picked it up and set it on his index finger, spinning it around.

" . . . there's more at stake here than you know. Come on, Big Daddy, it's almost Christmas. You have to understand. Show a little compassion."

Big Daddy's response was so loud that Pops didn't need to have the phone pressed against his ear to make it out. He could even hear the *click* on the other end as Big Daddy hung up on him.

Distraught, Pops pulled the phone away and hung up. He was just about to bury his face in his hands but settled on staring at Guido's hat instead, wondering if miracles really did happen.

A moment later A.J. came into the office, dressed in his hockey uniform.

"Is everything okay, Grandpa?"

Pops shook his head. He wished he could give A.J. a different answer—maybe at least some hope—but he couldn't. "No, unfortunately not. Big Daddy refuses to give me an extension on the lease, and I can't seem to get the money in time."

A.J. looked at his grandfather with big, watery eyes. "Big Daddy's really gonna close the Ice Palace?"

Pops pressed his lips together in a fine line. "I'm afraid it looks that way." He took in A.J.'s mournful expression. "Hey, cheer up, we have a game to play. What have we learned? If life gives you lemons . . ."

A.J. sniffled, straightening up. "Make lemonade."

Pops smiled. "That's my boy. Now, let's get you on the ice."

Together, they exited the office, making their way towards the ice and quite possibly a better future, completely unaware of the three pairs of eyes staring at them from the hole in the floor molding.

"I can't believe my ears," said Guido. "We're gonna lose the Ice Palace?"

"You don't know that for certain," said Gia. "You heard that man—he still has until Christmas to come up with the money."

"Gia's right," Nerdy agreed. "There's still a chance."

"But you heard him—the bank won't give him another loan. We can't just stand here while that Big Daddy guy closes the rink."

Gia looked at Guido, confused. "What do you mean?"

"I mean we have to do something!"

"Like what?" asked Nerdy. "These are human problems, and we're only rats."

"I don't know, but we can't lose the Ice Palace. We just can't."

"Then what do you suggest?" asked Gia.

Guido thought long and hard. "I don't know. But what I *do* know is that I'm gonna get my hat, we're gonna beat the Maulers, then the Canadians, and we're gonna save this rink! Tonight, at practice, we'll tell everyone what we heard and we'll put our heads together and come up with something."

With that, he leaped though the hole and scurried across the floor towards the desk.

"Guido, wait!"

Guido did no such thing. He reached the desk and clambered up the leg like a lumberjack. When he made it to the top, he weaved his way around a pile of papers, a stapler, a desk lamp, and a few other obstacles. In his preoccupation, he didn't see the open ink pad or the Brooklyn Ice Palace stamp. He crashed into these, stepping on the ink pad and tumbling over the stamp. When he got up, he left little purple footprints everywhere he stepped.

That was bad. What was even worse was that Pops Anderson walked back into the office.

Guido froze.

"I'll be right there!" Pops called over his shoulder. "I just gotta get my whistle!"

"Oh no!" Gia cried.

"Come on, Guido!" Nerdy whispered. "Get out of there!"

Instead of turning around, Guido made a break for his hat.

Gia shut her eyes.

Nerdy put his paws over his. "I can't watch."

It turned out they didn't have to worry—Guido snatched up the hat just in time and leaped off the edge of the desk. When he hit the floor, he high-tailed it out of there, racing towards the hole in the wall.

Pops froze. He was staring at the tiny footprints on his desk. His face twisted in confusion, trying to make sense of what he was seeing. He might have stood there, mouth agape, for the better of five minutes if movement hadn't caught his eye. Very slowly, he turned his head, taking in the sight of a little rat scurrying across the floor. And not just any rat—a rat wearing a green, white, and red hat.

"Wait!" Pops called out. He tried to move as fast as he could but the rat was faster. "Wait!"

The rat did no such thing. It dove into the hole in the wall and vanished.

Pops bent down, the joints of his knees popping like twin pistols. He winced at the pain this brought but carried on, lowering his head to the floor so he could peer into the hole.

There was nothing inside but blackness.

Chapter 12

The Brooklyn Ice Palace looked different at night than it did during the day. Because it was nearly midnight, none of the lights had been turned on in the lobby, creating a vast chasm of darkness. The pro shop remained empty and silent. The TVs dead and motionless. The only part that still had any life was the ice. Every other bulb on the ceiling remained lit, casting shadows about the room. Even though it was nowhere near as bright during operation hours, the bulbs still cast enough glow to illuminate the ice. It was by this light that the Brooklyn Rink Rats would play.

They sat beside their lockers in the locker room, their mouths open, shock written across their faces. Even Cream Puff, who stroked Oscar the Kitten as it lapped up a small bowl of milk, stared in a kind of fascinated stupor, his cream puffs temporarily forgotten.

" . . . we all heard him on the phone. He was talking to this guy named Big Daddy. Apparently if he doesn't pay Big Daddy the money he owes him, Big Daddy's gonna close the Ice

Palace. Forever . . ."

There were dejected mumbles throughout the room.

"Forever?" Marcello asked in his French accent.

"Forever," confirmed Nerdy. "There was no mistaking that part."

"What are we gonna do?" Sergio asked. His face was wrought with agitation. It was clear that he didn't want the rink to close.

"That's ridiculous," said Angelo. "Where are we gonna play? How are we gonna have a team?"

"There's always another team," said Patrick, his Irish brogue staining his voice.

"And we can always find another place to play," added his brother Brian.

Sergio didn't want to hear it. "No! The Ice Palace is our home! We're not going anywhere!"

"We need to figure this out," said Marcello. "There has to be a way."

"Yeah," said Nerdy, "there's always a way. We just need to put our heads together and come up with every plausible option. The odds are in our favor that one will work."

Cream Puff stood up, Oscar clutched tightly to his chest. "But what can we do? We're just rats."

"Aye," said Patrick. "And some of us are bigger than others." He chuckled, poking Cream Puff's belly as he said this.

Guido grinded his teeth together. He felt like pulling the hair out of his head. "Guys! This isn't funny. We have to take this seriously. We're gonna lose the rink if—"

"What we need to do," said a rat standing in the shadows, "is *win!*"

All heads swiveled in his direction. Coach Lucky stepped into the light.

"If this is gonna be our last chance to play at the Ice Palace, then we need to play some hockey. We need to beat the Maulers so we can play the Canadians."

Guido couldn't help but smile, happy that Lucky had made the right decision and shown up. He tipped him a wink. Lucky tipped him one back. Although Lucky felt a bit queasy when he did it, knowing that he had to make a decision on whether or not he was going to betray his team if they won. A very small part of him wanted them to lose so he wouldn't have to make it after all.

"Sounds good to me," said Sergio. He stood up and put his right paw out. "Who's in?"

"I am," said Marcello. He stuck his paw out and put it on top of Sergio's.

Angelo stood up next. "Me, too!"

"And so are we," said the O'Shaunessay brothers.

One by one the rats stood up, forming a circle and putting their paws in the center. Lucky was the last to add his. "And I'll be there with you guys every step of the way." His voice nearly caught in his throat when he said this. "What do you say? Go Rink Rats?"

Altogether, the cheer rose up, filling the locker room with motivation.

Motivation is a curious thing. Without it, one might not feel compelled to do his best, merely go through the actions instead. On the other hand, when infused with the urge to be the best, one usually tries to become even *better*. The Brooklyn Rink Rats practiced like they had never practiced before, running drills, making formations, passing, shooting, and most importantly encouraging each other every step of the way. Each rat used his strong-point to his advantage: Lucky and Nerdy went over strategies, Sergio and Angelo put those plays into practice, the O'Shaunessay brothers worked on stopping slap shots, and Cream Puff and Marcello checked each other, Cream Puff winning hands-down as poor Marcello bounced off his big belly. Even Oscar the Kitten got in on the fun. He wanted to join the rats so bad that he leaped onto the ice, unaware until it was too late that it was as slippery as can be. Almost as soon as he touched the surface, his feet went out from under him, sprawling every which way, forcing him to slide towards the goal on his belly. He crashed into Patrick O'Shaunessay, the rat poking his head out of the big ball of fur.

All in all, practice was a huge success. Now, if only the Rink Rats could play just as well tomorrow . . .

Chapter 13

The Brooklyn Rink Rats sat beside their lockers just as they had the night before. Even though they were sitting in the exact same formation, the mood was completely different. Instead of being quiet because of the story Guido and Nerdy were telling them, they were quiet because of the approaching game. Each rat sat in his own mind, psyching himself out, visualizing himself winning, getting ready to step onto the ice and become a champion.

Every rat was present, repeating the same drill. Every rat except Coach Lucky.

"Are you here?" Lucky whispered. The corridor outside the locker room was dark, like a cave. He hated having to creep around his own rink. It made him feel dirty. It also made him a bit nervous. He never knew if he was going to turn the wrong corner and stumble into a spider web, or quite possibly something even worse.

"Yes, I'm here . . ." said a voice.

Its owner stepped out from the shadows, a big rat with eyes

as red as fire and hair as pointy as nails. Two muscular rats accompanied him.

"Where else would I be?" Spike asked. "When there's money to be made, I'm always around." He cracked his knuckles. "Have you made a decision?"

Lucky reluctantly nodded. "I have."

"And . . . ?"

It was hard to say the words. He knew saying them would make him a horrible rat. His team trusted him. They were counting on him to bring them to victory against the Canadians. Only . . . Lucky's sick mother was counting on him, too. She needed the money to pay the overdue rent. For that reason, he bit his lip, hoping he wasn't making the biggest mistake of his life. "I'll do it."

Spike could barely contain his joy. He craned his head back and laughed, a sickly, chuckling sound. His henchmen echoed it, as if it were contagious, the sound carrying them off as they disappeared into the darkness.

"Good. You'll get the first half after the game." He added, "That is, if you win."

"Sorry I'm late," said Lucky, finally stepping into the locker room. "I had to take care of something. Are you guys ready to kick some butt?"

Guido frowned. He had a feeling he knew exactly what that *something* was.

"I'm ready!" said Sergio.

Marcello stood up. "Me, too!"

The rest of the rats joined in.

Lucky gave cry to the cheer: "Then let's get out there and win!"

Like a whirlwind, the Rink Rats surged out of the locker room, taking the ice by storm. Only two rats stayed behind.

"Is everything all right?" Guido asked, afraid of the answer.

Lucky could barely meet his eyes. "Do you really want the truth?"

Guido thought for a long time. "No . . . I guess I don't." He put a paw on his friend's shoulder. "We'll talk about this, I promise, but right now I need you to help us beat the Maulers. Can you do that?"

Lucky nodded. That, at least, was something he could do.

The Ice Palace was alive with vitality. Every type of rat occupied the stands: fans, friends, family, security, even vendor rats. They all gave a raucous cheer as the Rink Rats stepped on the ice.

Cream Puff's mother handed out cream puffs. Angelo's grandmother sounded a bullhorn. Nerdy's mother and father pressed their fingers in their ears as they cast side-long glances at the old woman. There was even a row of girls with sweatshirts that said *WE LOVE MARCELLO* across the front. Everyone was present, even Gia, who sat in the second row with Oscar. She had dressed the kitten in a hat and one of the extra Rink Rats' jerseys, hoping it would disguise the fact that he was a cat. It seemed to be working because nobody was running for their lives.

The Rink Rats skated around, warming up, passing and shooting when one of the many warm-up pucks came their way. On the other side of the ice, the Manhattan Maulers did the same. They wore yellow and black uniforms with black helmets, resembling angry hornets ready to sting. They might have looked intimidating to some, but Guido saw the one rat he was truly afraid of.

Sneaking in from the side of the stands, preparing to spy on the game and gather information to take back to his team, was Pierre La'Monte, the captain of the Canadians. He was as arrogant as they came. Tall and lean with a long nose, Pierre stood out from the others. Or maybe he had his red and white team-colored jacket or the red beret to thank for that. It didn't matter. What mattered was that he was here.

The fans who recognized him booed loudly.

Pierre paid them no attention. He made his way to the ice and motioned for Guido to skate over.

"Well, well," said Pierre, "we meet again, Monsieur Guido."

"It would appear that way, wouldn't it?" Guido tried to compose himself as best he could. Inside he was shaking.

"Tell you what, why don't you give up now and let the Mauler's play us. They would be more competition anyway."

Guido tried to puff out his chest. "Do I sense somebody who's nervous?"

Pierre chuckled, an irritating high-pitched sound that echoed in the open space of the rink. "I believe you're sensing yourself. Believe me, if I were you, and I knew I might be playing the Canadians, I'd be nervous, too."

"You should really be careful—that ego of yours might burst."

Pierre wasted no time in replying. "An ego rightfully earned."

Guido had had enough. He didn't need to stand here talking to this rat. "Excuse me, I have a game to win. Why don't you go take a seat and watch us earn our way into the championships." He thought for a second. "Tell you what, you can watch us win that, too, since you'll be on the ice when it happens."

With that, he skated away. Pierre shouted something after him, but it was lost in the cheers of the crowd.

Chapter 14

It would be exciting to say that the hockey game was galvanizing, electric even, both teams shooting goals one after the other, the score tied with barely any time left on the clock.

That wasn't the case at all. It was true that there were only two minutes left in the third and last period, but not a single team had scored. That didn't mean the game wasn't exciting, though. Quite the contrary. It had been exhilarating, the fans on the edge of their seats the whole time. The Rink Rats had stolen the puck from the Maulers and the Maulers had stolen it right back. Back and forth they had gone, playing some incredible defense and shooting on each other's goal. Both goalies played an unbelievable game. Rivers of sweat dripped down their brows from their effort. It seemed that neither of them would let a single puck in the net.

That was all great for the Rink Rats, but they needed to step up their offense if they wanted to win.

Angelo skated hard down the ice, Guido on his left. He maneuvered around a Mauler defenseman. He passed the puck to Guido, and Guido passed it back after skating around the second defenseman. Angelo wasted no time. He shot the puck as hard as he could. It cut through the air like a bullet, heading right for the top-left corner of the net.

The Maulers' goalie was fast. With a flick of his wrist, he caught the puck.

"Time out!" Lucky shouted.

All the Rink Rats skated over to the bench.

"Their goalie's good," said Angelo.

"Real good," added Guido.

Patrick scuffed. "He's good, but not as good as me."

"Or me, since I'm slightly better than you," Brian chimed in with a smirk on his face.

"It doesn't matter which one of you is better," said Lucky. "What matters is that we haven't scored and there's less than two minutes on the clock. We need to do something, and we need to do it fast."

Nerdy skated over, a clipboard in his paw. "I have an idea."

Lucky took it, studying the play. Slowly, his lips turned up in a smile. "This might just work."

The timeout ended and the game resumed, Guido and a Mauler meeting center ice. The referee dropped the puck, and the two fought for it. After some heavy struggling, Guido won possession. He passed the puck to Angelo without a second to spare.

"Brian, now!" Lucky called out.

Brian skated out of the Rink Rat's net and headed towards the bench. Immediately, Cream Puff and Sergio retreated to protect it. That was Nerdy's cue: he leaped off the bench and joined the Rink Rats for a power play.

Angelo dropped back and passed the puck to Nerdy. Nerdy accepted the pass and passed it to Marcello. Marcello then passed it to Guido.

While all this distraction was going on, Angelo skated for the Maulers' net, a single Mauler defenseman chasing after him.

Guido smacked the puck to Angelo. Angelo skated hard. When he caught up to it, he stick-handled the puck towards the goal, the blade with the three stripes of red tape on it a blur.

The clock ticked down, the Mauler defenseman hot on his heels. When he was as close as he dared to get, Angelo pulled his stick back and hit the puck as hard as he could. The defenseman couldn't let him get away with it. He checked him with all the force he could muster. At this point, several things happened at the same time: Angelo's blade shattered, the puck soared through the air like a rocket ship, the crowd stood up and cheered, and the Maulers' goalie threw himself over to the side of the net to block the shot. In all the commotion, nobody saw Angelo's leg twist as he hit the ice.

The next few seconds felt like they took forever. As if in slow-motion, everyone watched the puck inch its way toward the goal. The Maulers goalie's glove came up. Instead of catching the puck, it brushed up against it. Then, all at once, time snapped and everything sped back up. The puck wobbled, flipping end over end, and sailed into the top-right corner of the net.

The cheer that erupted was deafening. One by one, the Rink Rats bounded off the bench to join their team on the ice. They all hugged in a cheerful embrace. All except for Angelo.

"Are you okay?" Guido asked, hurriedly skating over to him.

Angelo writhed in pain, holding his knee. "No, I can't get up. My knee . . ."

Chapter 15

Angelo sat on a bench in the locker room with his leg propped up on a stool. A large ice pack sat on his knee like a cherry on a sundae. An older rat with gray hair and a white coat knelt down beside him, a stethoscope dangling from his neck as he inspected the injury.

"Well, the good thing is it doesn't appear to be broken," said the doctor.

That was a relief. "Will I still be able to play?" Angelo asked.

The doctor rubbed his chin. "I don't see why not. You're just going to have to wait for it to heal first."

"How long will that take?" Guido asked.

The doctor thought for a moment. "I would give it about six to eight weeks to be safe."

"Six to eight weeks?" Angelo shouted. "But we're playing the Canadians in two days!"

Guido gave him a harsh stare. "Not with that leg you're not."

"Come on, Guido, I have to! I can't just sit around and let you guys down."

"But you didn't let us down."

"He's right," said Nerdy. "If it wasn't for you, we might not be playing the Canadians at all. You did your part for sure."

"I guess," said Angelo, "but I'd still really like to play them."

Guido couldn't help but laugh. "I bet you do. The important thing is for you to get better. You'll still be with us every step of the way."

"How are you feeling?" asked Cream Puff, coming over to join them.

Angelo looked at his swollen knee. "To tell the truth, I've been in better shape."

"Maybe this will make you feel better?" He turned around and brought out a surprise. Oscar the Kitten was cradled in his arms, a big ball of fur in a Rink Rats hat and jersey.

Angelo couldn't help but laugh.

"You're right," he said. "That does make me feel a little better. I guess we really do have a cat for a mascot. Who would have thought?"

While all was cheerful in the locker room, the atmosphere was a bit more bleak in the dark hallway outside. A familiar rat with spiked hair and red eyes loomed in the shadows, glaring at Lucky.

"This is yours." He reached into his pocket and pulled out a wad of cash. Before handing it to Lucky, Spike held it up to his noise and breathed in deeply, his whole body shuddering. For a moment—a *long* moment—the wad of cash just sat in Spike's paw. Finally, he handed it over, his fingers slowly unhinging as if they needed oil to work. "It pains me to have to give this up. However, knowing that you're going to make me a very rich rat is my only solace."

Lucky clutched the money like a life preserver. It was just enough to pay his sick mother's rent. He quickly stuffed it into his jersey, fearing Spike might change his mind and ask for it back.

"You'll get the rest on Christmas Eve," Spike said. "You know what to do. Final score: Canadians 4, Rink Rats 1. Got it?"

Lucky felt a lump growing in his throat. "I got it."

Spike grinned. "Do I dare say it? Good luck . . ."

Laughing maniacally, he turned tail and threw open the door, disappearing outside into the falling snow.

"What was that about?" a voice asked from down the hall. It belonged to Patrick O'Shaunessay. He walked up, his brother Brian not too far behind.

Lucky tried to compose himself. "Nothing."

Brian gave him an incredulous look. "Didn't seem like nothing. Who was that anyway?"

"Yeah," Patrick chimed in. "That rat looked like he meant business. He didn't threaten you, did he?"

"'Cause if he did," Brian added, cracking his knuckles, "Patrick and I here could set him straight."

"I'm fine," said Lucky. "It was nothing."

Patrick shrugged. "If you say so." He might have said more, but a big furry paw from outside reached in through the door and grabbed him around the waist.

"Got ya!" said Sid the Alley Cat. "Finally, a late-night snack." He pulled Brian towards him. "And by the looks of it, a nice-sized one, too."

Patrick didn't miss a beat. The moment Sid grabbed hold of his brother he leaped out the door after him. "Put my brother down, you big fur ball!"

Sid eyed the second rat, his mouth watering. "What do we have here? Desert?"

"No," Patrick roared, "your worst nightmare!" With that, he lunged at Sid, punching, kicking, and scratching.

In all his life Sid never had a rat try to beat him up. Perhaps that's why it took him by total surprise. Caught off guard, he dropped Brian and held up his paws to defend himself.

The moment Brian was free, he joined in the fight, leaping

onto Sid's back, pulling the cat's ears and biting them.

Lucky knew better than to try to fight the cat—he'd already tested his luck once this night. That's why he chose to run to the locker room instead.

"Help!" he cried, bursting through the door. *"Sid's outside! Brian and Patrick are fighting him!"*

None of the rats asked if this was a joke. They could tell by the tone of Lucky's voice that he was dead serious. All at once, they leaped up, rushing out of the locker room to help. The commotion startled Oscar the Kitten, who was curled up cozily in Cream Puff's lap. One moment he was fast asleep, the next he sprang up, bolting out the door.

"Oscar, no!" Cream Puff cried.

He rushed after the kitten, down the dark hall and out the open door into the night. There, he paused, staring at the sight before him.

Sid the Alley Cat, the dreaded terror of the night, was in an all-out brawl with the O'Shaunessay brothers. Tangled within this mess was Oscar, growling and scratching the larger cat every chance he got. To Cream Puff's disbelief, Sid was losing! The larger cat cried and whimpered, frantically trying to escape. He might have succeeded, but each time he tried, one of the O'Shaunessay brothers grabbed his tail and pulled him back into the melee.

"That'll teach you to try to eat us!" Brian shouted.

"Yeah!" yelled Patrick. "How do *you* like it?" He opened his mouth nice and wide and bit down on Sid's tail as hard as he could.

If Sid's cries had been loud before, this one was absolutely deafening. It shattered the night, reverberating in the still air. It gave Sid enough energy to coil his back legs under him and spring forward. Brian and Patrick let him go. They watched the evil cat streak off into the night, a big blur of fur.

The only one who didn't let him go this easily was Oscar. The kitten took off after him, racing past the sidewalk and into the street.

Cream Puff was the only one to see the truck coming.

"No! Oscar! Come back!" He didn't think. He ran right into the street after him.

The truck slammed on its brakes. The high-pitched screeching sound froze Oscar in his tracks. The poor little kitten stood in the middle of the road, glaring with fright as the bright headlights bore down on him.

"Oscar!"

Cream Puff leaped, his arms held out in front of him. They pushed Oscar out of the way at the last possible second. Only . . . Cream Puff wasn't so lucky.

The loud thump echoed in the night. The truck passed to reveal Cream Puff's motionless body lying on the cold, hard pavement. His hockey jersey was in tatters, red splotches everywhere.

The Rink Rats raced over to him.

"Somebody call an ambulance!" Guido shouted. He tapped Cream Puff on his puffy cheeks, hoping to wake the rat up. Cream Puff didn't move. "Call an ambulance! Quick!"

Not even little Oscar licking his paws could wake him.

Chapter 16

The next night the Rink Rats found themselves in their locker room crying. It seemed that not even a good practice could lighten their mood. All their eyes were swollen and red, and they kept wandering over to the corner, where Oscar lay curled up on Cream Puff's red vest, sad and dejected.

Angelo tucked his head into his arm and sobbed. He sat in a wheelchair, a red cast on his right leg. All his teammates had signed it. All except for Cream Puff . . .

Finally, Guido spoke, breaking the silence.

"Tonight was a good practice, guys. I know it was hard, especially under the circumstances." He looked towards the corner, shedding a tear. "But Cream Puff would have wanted us to practice. He would have wanted us to be ready to beat the Canadians."

There were silent nods all around the room.

"I'm going by the church after I change. I'm gonna say a prayer for Cream Puff. Anybody's welcome to join me."

Several of the rats lifted their heads, their moods lightening.

"I'll go," said Sergio.

Marcello stood up. "Me, too. A prayer sounds like the right thing."

"I'll talk to the almighty," said Patrick.

"Same," added Brian.

Nerdy nodded. "A prayer would definitely be a good idea."

Lucky agreed that he'd go, but he didn't say much. He mostly kept to himself, trying not to interact with the friends he was about to betray.

Angelo wheeled himself to the center of the room. "I'd love to go with you guys, but it'd take me forever to get there. I think I'm gonna stay here with Oscar instead." He turned to Guido. "Will you say a prayer for me?"

Guido gave a tiny smile. "Of course."

Marcello clapped his paws together. "Then it's settled. To the church!"

The church, majestic and resplendent, was a marvel of architecture. Huge spires twisted their way to the heavens, large beautiful stained glass windows decorated the facade, and fine hand-carved crosses adorned the long glowing aisles. The atmosphere inside was warm and inviting. Flickering candles under the statues of saints beckoned rats forward. Deep red carpets called others down the aisles. And thick, plushy cushions invited others to the pews to pray.

One by one, the Rink Rats ushered themselves down an aisle and into a pew. There they sat for the better of fifteen minutes, sending out their prayers for Cream Puff.

As they exited the church, Nerdy caught sight of the nativity scene on the front lawn. The other rats continued to walk, but Nerdy stopped in front of it, taking notice of the baby Jesus inside the crib. Underneath the statue lay a bed of straw.

Nerdy looked around surreptitiously. When he was sure that nobody was watching, he crept forward and pulled out a paw-full.

"Hey, what are you doing?"

Nerdy nearly jumped out of his skin. He spun around to find Guido behind him.

"What? Umm, nothing."

Guido looked at the straw in his teammate's paw. "Doesn't look like nothing to me."

Nerdy figured it couldn't hurt to tell the truth. "My grandmother's really big on miracles. She told me that the straw underneath the baby Jesus is blessed. She said that if you carry it around and say a prayer a miracle will happen."

Guido raised his eyebrows, skeptical. "That can't be true. If it is, everybody would be taking the straw."

"That's just it," said Nerdy, "you have to *truly* believe in order for it to work."

"Do *you* believe?"

Nerdy raised his paw, rubbing the straw gently against his cheek. "I do."

Chapter 17

There were crumbs on the counter top. Guido barely noticed. He had so many things on his mind that he just stared out the window of the pizzeria watching the snow fall. The rag in his paw dangled limply by his side.

Gia walked in, stomping her boots and shaking the snow off her hat. "'Morning, Guido! Merry Christmas Eve!"

Guido continued to stare off into the distance, oblivious of his surroundings.

Gia cleared her throat and repeated herself, this time a little louder.

Guido shook his head and blinked, noticing Gia for the first time. "Oh! Right, yeah, merry Christmas Eve to you, too."

Gia hung up her coat and pulled off her hat. The hair underneath, usually straight and plain—although still beautiful—fell down in lustrous curly plaits. She shook her head, making them rock from one shoulder to the other.

When Guido didn't say anything, she frowned and came around the counter. She looked at the papers by the cash register and picked one up, trying her best to keep up the good mood she'd walked in with. "Only one order for today. Looks like a catering tray for Mr. O'Brien. After this we have a whole week off. Aren't you excited?"

"Huh? Yeah. Great." Guido looked at her for all of two seconds then went back to staring out the window. He couldn't help but think about all the bad luck his team was having. First off, they were going to lose the rink. Second, they were down two players: Cream Puff got hit by a truck and Angelo couldn't play because of his leg. To top it all off, they had to somehow manage to focus enough to beat the Canadians tonight. He had no idea what they were going to do.

"I got you a Christmas present," Gia said. She nuzzled up to Guido, summoning the courage to get as close as she dared— close enough so he could finally realize that she liked him more than just a friend.

She batted her eyelashes. "Did you get me anything?"

Guido only continued to stare out the window, ignoring her.

Gia took a step back, afraid she might have pushed her limits. "Guido?"

Guido blinked again. "What?"

Gia frowned. "Never mind." She didn't know what was wrong with him. Guido had never acted this way, especially around her. Usually he was all giddy or even shy, stumbling over his words in that cute way she liked. Now he was flat-out ignoring her. She didn't know if she'd done something wrong, or if he didn't like the special way she'd done her hair today, or worse . . .

What if he didn't like her anymore?

Needing to know, Gia tried one more time to get him to talk. "Are you nervous about the game tonight?"

Guido tossed the rag on the counter. "What's with all the questions, Gia? Can't you see I'm thinking?"

That did it. "Fine!" Gia shouted. "I won't talk to you then!" She stormed out the room, disappearing into the back and slamming the door leading outside.

A minute later a loud banging sound issued forth from the alley behind the pizzeria.

Guido threw up his paws, rolling his eyes. "Now what?"

He stalked into the back, following Gia's path. When he opened the door leading out into the alley, he paused.

Gia was standing amidst a scatter of charcoal, holding a hockey stick. She pulled it back and slammed it forward, striking one of the pieces. It sailed through the air and violently shattered against the inside of a tipped-over garbage pail.

Only then did Guido notice the little red bow tied ornately around the shaft.

"Gia?" he asked, cautiously.

Gia spun around, fuming. *"What?"*

Guido took a small step back. "What are you doing?"

"What does it look like I'm doing? I'm pretending the charcoal's your head, and I'm smacking it to smithereens with the stick I bought you because you're being a jerk!"

That made Guido pause. He *did* feel like a jerk. But he also paused for another reason. Cautiously, he asked, "I'm sorry, my mind's been going a mile a minute, but where did you learn to shoot like that?"

Now it was Gia's turn to pause. "My dad. He always wanted a boy. He taught me everything he knows about hockey. Including . . ." She brought the stick back and slammed it against another piece of charcoal, sending it careening into the back of the pail, where it burst into a million pieces. ". . . how to shoot."

Guido's jaw dropped open.

"What?" Gia asked.

Guido ventured to ask the next question, silently praying the answer was yes. "Can you skate?"

Gia nodded. "Yeah, why?"

That put a huge smile on Guido's face. "I think I have an idea."

Chapter 18

New York-Presbyterian was a big building off 68th Street and New York Avenue. It was so big that it spanned the whole block and sat against the East River. In fact, it was one of the nation's largest and most comprehensive hospitals. It was also home to some of the best doctors in the world.

Deep in the basement, in a wing long forgotten by the humans when the hospital was remodeled, sat the Rat Ward. Like the hospital above, it was a flurry of activity.

Inside the waiting room, dozens of concerned rats sat in chairs or paced back and forth. Nurses dressed in green scrubs with their tails poking out the back jostled down bright hallways. Rats in white coats with stethoscopes dangling from their necks scribbled things on clipboards. If there a disease, they were working frantically to cure it. If there was an injury, they wasted no time in healing it.

Nerdy took all of this in as he entered the intensive care unit in the Rat Ward. To his surprise, there wasn't a waiting room here. Instead, there were a bunch of rooms branching off the hallway. He peeked into one of them. A big white hospital bed sat in the center with an old rat lying in it. About a million beeping machines surrounded it. Nerdy quickly pulled his head back, moving to the next room.

In this one he found a little girl rat sitting up in the bed. Her parents were beside her holding her paw. The little girl rat looked sad.

Nerdy kept walking.

Finally he came to a room at the end of the hall. He took one look in and knew this was the room he'd been looking for.

Very slowly, he approached the bed. His sneakers made little squeaking sounds on the polished floor. As he walked, he pulled some of the blessed straw out of his pocket. He opened the patient's paw and placed the straw inside.

"This is for you, Cream Puff."

The straw slipped out and Nerdy had to put it back in, this time closing Cream Puff's paw around it. The action brought tears to his eyes.

"Get better, please. The team misses you. Oscar misses you. We're taking good care of him, so don't worry." He paused, sniffling. "I wish you could just wake up."

This was hard. Nerdy had never been to the hospital before, and seeing Cream Puff lying so helplessly in the bed was heartbreaking.

"I brought you a gift. It's straw from under the baby Jesus.

My grandmother says it's blessed and can make a miracle happen. Do you know what? If I had one wish, it wouldn't be for us to beat the Canadians. It'd be for you to wake up and be okay."

He gave Cream Puff's paw a big squeeze and turned to leave.

An almost inaudible voice made him turn back around. It was rough, hoarse, and barely above a whisper, but Nerdy knew that voice just the same.

"Cream Puff?"

He stared at his friend lying motionlessly in the bed. Cream Puff was so still that he looked like a statue. There was no way he could have talked. Nerdy had been so hopeful that for a second he'd almost believed he'd heard something. Sometimes the imagination could play tricks on you like that.

Disappointed, he turned to leave again. This time he got all the way to the door before he heard it again.

"Nerdy . . . ?"

Nerdy spun around, sure he'd heard his name this time.

Cream Puff stirred.

Nerdy rushed over to his bedside. "Cream Puff!"

Cream Puff parted his eyes, his eyelids fluttering like wings.

"Nurse! Nurse!" Nerdy was up at once, screaming down the hallway. He needed somebody to come quick.

"W-what happened?"

Nerdy made his way over to the bed again. "You had an

accident. There was a truck and—"

Cream Puff seemed to remember. "Is Oscar okay? He ran out into the street."

"He's fine," Nerdy reassured him.

Cream Puff smiled. "Good." He looked around the room. "Where are all the guys?"

Hearing Cream Puff's voice with so much strength in it brought tears to Nerdy's eyes.

"They're back at the rink. It's Christmas Eve. They're getting ready for the game against the Canadians."

"What?" Cream Puff shouted, horrified. "Why are you here?"

"What do you mean? I came to see you."

"I mean, thank you and all. That was really nice of you, but go! The team needs you! Don't worry about me. I'll be fine."

Nerdy regarded his friend with unadulterated jubilation. "I know you will. We're gonna win this one for you."

Cream Puff clutched the straw. "I don't have any doubt."

Chapter 19

The crowd that had gathered was so big that Guido could hear them cheering for the game against the Canadians to start even from within the locker room. He paced back and forth, glancing at the clock each time, wondering where Nerdy could be. This was a disaster. He'd found a temporary replacement for Cream Puff, but now *Nerdy* was missing! He had no idea how the team could pull through without the brains behind the plays.

He made one more circuit across the locker room before throwing his paws up. "That's it! Are you guys sure nobody's seen Nerdy?"

The locker room door crashed open, Nerdy standing in its frame. "I'm here! I'm here!"

Guido felt like fainting with relief. "Where were you?"

Nerdy didn't hold back. "At the hospital. Guys, Cream Puff's awake! He's okay!"

Everyone did a double take. Some stood up.

"Cream Puff's okay?"

"He's awake?"

"He's gonna make it?"

"Yes!" Nerdy shouted, his voice barely audible above his friends' surprised cries.

"It's a miracle!" Marcello blurted out.

Brian and Patrick high-fived each other.

"What happened?" Guido asked when everyone calmed down.

Nerdy said, "I put the straw I took from the church in his paw, and he just woke up!"

"I knew he'd be okay!" Angelo said from his wheelchair as he stroked Oscar. He bent down toward the kitten. "He's gonna be okay, Oscar. See, I told you."

Oscar purred loudly and shot out his little pink tongue, licking Angelo's face.

Lucky was the only one to act different: he stayed quiet, keeping to himself. Inside his head his conscience screamed at him. This was his *team*, his *second family*, and he was going to betray them? He found that he was so sick with what he had agreed to do that he couldn't even bring himself to look at his teammates. Especially Guido, who had been there for him more times than he could count. Guido, who checked up on him to make sure he was okay; Guido, who let him join the team; and Guido, who gave him the opportunity to be the coach while he very well could have done the job himself. The betrayal made Lucky feel horrible, yet he had to go through with it. He had no other choice. Even if he wanted to back down, he couldn't—Spike's henchmen would never let him see the light of day again.

"Wait . . ." Sergio said, cutting into his thoughts. "We're still down a player."

The mood in the locker room darkened. The Rink Rats knew they couldn't beat the Canadians without a full team.

Guido betrayed the hint of a smile. "I was waiting to tell you guys. I found a replacement."

They all looked at him with impatient anticipation.

"Who?" Brian asked.

"Yeah, who?" Angelo repeated.

"Hold on just a sec." Guido slipped out the door. When he returned, he was holding Gia's paw.

Everyone looked, confused.

"Gia?" Patrick asked. "But she's a girl. No offense."

Gia only laughed. "None taken." She stepped up proudly to the center of the locker room. "Yes, as a matter of fact I *am* a girl, but that doesn't mean I can't play hockey."

"It's true," Guido said. "She's got one of the best slap shots I've ever seen."

Sergio said, "Can't be better than mine."

Guido didn't miss a beat. "If it isn't, then it certainly comes close. Guys, we all need to work together to win this one. Since Gia's graciously accepted the offer to play tonight, I think we all owe her our gratitude."

"She definitely gets mine," Nerdy said.

Angelo agreed. "And mine! Thank you, Gia."

Gia smiled. "It's my pleasure."

There might have been more thanks given, but a low rumbling shook the walls. All the Rink Rats froze.

The Canadians.

One by one, they made their way out of the locker room and to a window in the hallway. Sure enough, a big silver bus with a red maple leaf emblazoned on the side pulled up, puffing smoke in the cold air. The door opened and a familiar rat stepped out.

Pierre La'Monte, the captain of the Canadians, was impossible to miss with his red and white team-colored jacket and the red beret perched pompously on his head.

"Come on, everybody out, we have a game to win. Are you rats or are you mice!"

The rats that stepped off the bus were twice the size of the Rink Rats. It honestly looked like they had gotten bigger since the last time the Rink Rats had played them. Mean and unfriendly, they wore the guises of executioners. Several of them were chewing what might have been gum, although it wouldn't have surprised the Rink Rats if it was nails instead, that's how tough they looked.

Nerdy swallowed. "Are you guys ready?" he asked, his voice shaky.

Patrick and Brian cracked their knuckles. "We were born ready. Let's beat these babies!"

Guido looked at Gia, studying her slender frame. "Maybe this isn't such a good idea . . ."

"Can it." She grabbed her stick, clutching it like a sledge hammer. "The bigger they are, the harder they fall."

"Here, here!" shouted Brian and Patrick in unison. "That's the spirit! Let's show them who the real champions are!"

As they filed out, Guido tapped Nerdy on the shoulder. "Would you mind taking Cream Puff's position tonight? Gia should take Angelo's."

"She's that good?" Nerdy asked.

Guido grinned. "She's got a slap shot hard enough to break glass."

Nerdy straightened his glasses, taking in the last of the Canadians as they stepped off the bus. "Good. It looks like we're gonna need it."

Chapter 20

Nerdy stopped dead in his tracks, halfway to the locker room.

Guido nearly bumped into him. "What's wrong?"

Nerdy hit himself in the forehead with the palm of his paw. "I almost forgot! There's something I have to do. Something really important. I'll be back before the game starts. I promise."

"Wait, what is it?"

"Never mind that," Nerdy called over his shoulder. "Just think positive thoughts about the game tonight. It's all about miracles!"

Guido looked confused, but Nerdy didn't stick around long enough to explain. He hurried off, scurrying through a hole in the wall. When he popped out, he was in Pops Anderson's office.

Without the desk lamp on to illuminate the room, it was dark and foreboding. The distant street lights outside shed some light through the window, causing eerie shadows to dance and creep across the walls as the wind howled and shook the trees.

Nerdy steeled himself, drawing up courage. He tiptoed out of the hole in the wall, ignoring the shadows as best he could, knowing he had a mission to accomplish.

When he reached the legs of the desk, he clambered up. On the surface were a clutter of papers, each one having to do with the rink and the financial problems Pops faced.

"This has to work," Nerdy said to himself. He reached into his pocket and pulled out the remainder of the blessed straw. Knowing everybody could use a miracle, he placed it under Pops Anderson's pen holder, where the old man would surely find it.

Chapter 21

The crowed roared as the Rink Rats stepped onto the ice. The rink was twice as packed as the time they played the Maulers. It seemed as if everyone in Little Rataly had come out to cheer them on this time. Half the fans were sporting either American or Italian flags, waving them so ferociously that one might have thought a huge fan had been turned on. The other half held brightly colored signs. Marcello's fan club stood front and center, their number easily doubled, their bright pink shirts with *WE LOVE MARCELLO* printed on them standing out in stark contrast against everything else. Angelo's grandmother sounded her bullhorn like always, this time joined by several others, melding together to create a cacophony of support.

The fans issued a loud *Boo!* as the foreign team made its way onto the ice. If camaraderie was all it took to win games, then the Canadians had no chance. Unfortunately this was not the case. The Rink Rats knew just as well as anyone else that the winner of this game would depend on skill alone. They just hoped they had practiced enough.

As the teams were warming up, Pierre La'Monte, the captain of the Canadians, skated over to Coach Lucky.

"You sure you want to go through with this, aye?" he said cockily.

Lucky gritted his teeth. He wanted to beat the Canadians and put Pierre in his place more than ever, but he knew he had to throw the game instead. It killed him inside because this time he actually believed his team had what it took to beat them.

Pierre chuckled, a merry, arrogant sound. "What's the matter? Cat got your tongue?" He looked around, surveying the Rink Rats. When he came upon Gia, he did a double take. "A girl? Is your team so desperate that you had to let a girl play?"

Lucky tensed up, feeling every muscle in his body twitch. "Just so you know, that girl has more talent in her tail than you do in your entire body."

This must have been the funniest thing Pierre had ever heard because he absolutely roared laugher. Now Lucky felt like jumping on top of him and beating him up. Knowing he just might do it, he decided it would be best to skate away.

Guido had never seen the Ice Palace so packed before. It seemed as if every seat was taken. There were even rats crouching and standing in the aisles, determined to watch the game. Guido scanned the crowd, taking in the wonder. A horrible chill raced down his spine. There, all the way in the back, sitting beside two beefy-looking rats, sat a rat in a black velvet suit with spiky hair. Guido didn't need binoculars to know that he had glaring red eyes. He'd seen this rat before and knew exactly what his presence implied.

He was just about to find Lucky, needing to talk with him, when Nerdy raced onto the ice, dressed in his regular clothes.

"I made it!"

Guido let out a sigh of relief. Not a full sigh—he had way too much tension built up to release it all—but a small sigh nonetheless. "Where did you go?"

Nerdy reached into his pocket and pulled out what remained of the blessed straw. "Miracles. I went to get us some miracles."

"The only miracle we need right now is to beat the Canadians." Guido looked back over to Spike. *And to save Lucky from whatever mess he got himself into this time,* he added under his breath.

Nerdy gave him a wink. "The miracles are on their way." With a flick of his wrist, he ripped his clothes off, exposing his hockey uniform beneath. "All we have to do now is believe . . ."

Chapter 22

The players took their positions on the ice. This trivial routine caused the crowd to go wild, since it implied the game was starting.

Guido took center ice, Marcello to his left, Gia to his right. Sergio and Nerdy stood behind them, preparing to give assistance any way they could. Defending the net, taking it all in through his caged mask, crouched Patrick O'Shaunessay, his brother Brian waiting patiently on the bench for his turn.

On the other side of the ice, the Canadians mirrored the Rink Rats' positions, Pierre directly across from Guido. Guido ignored the arrogant sneer on the rat's face and glanced over to Gia.

Not only did she look cute in the uniform with her long hair flowing out of the back of her helmet like a golden waterfall, but she looked prepared, as well. She crouched down, gripping her stick, chewing on her mouthpiece, ready to play some serious hockey. That's what Guido needed to see. It gave him the confidence to turn his head and glare right back at that arrogant face in front of him.

"Bonjour, Monsieur," Pierre said, grinning.

Guido grinned right back. "Can it. Let's play some hockey."

There was no time for a response. The referee dropped the puck and both rats jerked forward, digging at the ice. Guido managed to lean in and push Pierre back with his shoulder just enough to get control of the puck and tap it to Marcello.

Marcello didn't waste any time. He took the puck and danced by the Canadian player in front of him using an intricate volley of moves. He took it wide to the left and passed it to Gia.

That was the break the Rink Rats were waiting for. Gia had a lane, and she took it, pushing the puck up along the way, skating as fast as she could, Pierre hot on her heels. The rat was fast. *Very* fast. In the time it took Gia to look from the puck to the net, Pierre had skated up alongside her. He gave her a quick nod, grinned arrogantly, and dropped his hip. The next thing she knew she was flying hard into the boards.

The crowd booed.

Guido watched this from a few feet away, torn with what to do. Part of him wanted to skate over to Gia and make sure she was okay while the other wanted to go after Pierre.

Gia spared him the trouble of having to decide. She sat up and shook her first at Pierre. "Get him!"

Guido dug hard, digging his blades into the ice, Marcello right beside him.

Sergio and Nerdy switched gears, skating backwards, keeping their eyes trained on Pierre as he skated towards them.

Pierre faked a shot and Sergio dropped a knee, ready to throw his body in front of the puck if necessary. Pierre laughed and skated around him.

Nerdy wasn't fooled that easily. He might have made it over to Pierre, but he got checked by one of the Canadians.

In the net, Patrick tapped his stick against each post, psyching himself out. He crouched low, raising his glove as Pierre closed in. Pierre wound up, faked a slap shop, and instead pulled the puck far to the right and executed a wrist shot.

Patrick faltered, seeing his mistake at the last moment.

It was too late. The puck slid past his blocker and into the net.

The Canadian fans went wild. The Rink Rats' fans responded with a resonating *Booooo!*

Guido skated up to Gia, helping her up. "Are you okay?"

Gia brushed the ice off her jersey. "I'm fine." She glared at the Canadians with malice. "Thanks. Let's make them pay for that."

Coach Lucky looked up into the crowd. One would have thought it would be impossible to find someone in that screaming hodgepodge of fans. Spike, however, stood out like a sore thumb, seated calmly next to his two henchmen as the fans jumping around him screamed their aspersions at the Canadians.

Spike fixed his red eyes on Lucky. The two stared at one

another, locked in a visual embrace. Spike nodded. Lucky drew in a deep breath and nodded back. It felt like he was having trouble catching his breath. He felt even worse when he blew his whistle and called for a time out.

"Everybody to the bench!"

The rats on the ice skated over. All of Lucky's usual enthusiasm was gone. What remained was a dull, regretful ache. He could barely meet his teammates' gaze, especially when he pulled out his clipboard and tapped on the play that would cause them to give up the next goal.

Sure enough, when the game resumed, Pierre easily stole the puck. He circled back around his net, keeping it deep in his zone.

Marcello would have none of that. He skated right for the Canadian captain. When all the Rink Rats were in the Canadians' zone, Pierre dumped the puck. One of his players picked it up, skated to the net, and took a shot.

There was only one Rink Rat in the defensive zone. Lucky had told the team during the time out that if that happened, the defenseman had to stand directly in front of the goalie. Sergio didn't think that was the smartest of moves, but Lucky was the captain, and he knew what he was doing.

"Get outa the way!" Patrick shouted.

Sergio did no such thing. He stood where Lucky had told him to, unwittingly screening the net.

By then it was already too late. Not being able to see, Patrick dove the wrong way. The puck hit the net and the buzzer sounded, announcing to the fans that the Canadians had scored.

Sergio slammed his stick on the ice, breaking the blade. "I don't believe it!" he yelled. "We can't lose! Not again!"

Several of his teammates on the bench echoed his anger, punching the glass and tipping over the garbage pail.

Lucky shied away, wishing he could pull his head into his jersey like a tortoise does into its shell.

Chapter 23

Guido looked at the puck, wondering where the time had gone. One second it had been the first period and the Canadians had been leading 2 to 0, the next it was the third and the Canadians had scored twice more.

Even if he couldn't remember the time passing, he could remember the goals: It was Pierre who had managed to slip the puck between Patrick's legs, letting it slide right through the five-hole for a cheap goal. It had happened by accident, which was probably why Patrick had failed to stop it.

Pierre had succeeded in once more getting the puck into the Rink Rats' zone. Sergio and Nerdy converged on the rat like eagles attacking their prey. Pierre wavered, looking for a teammate to pass the puck to. When he realized his whole team was behind him, Pierre decided to charge the Rink Rats. Unprepared for such a move, Nerdy stumbled, tripping Pierre in the process. The Canadian crashed to the ice, the puck skidding wildly out of control. If they had been a bit farther down the ice, Patrick might have been able to stop it. As it was, they were only a foot away from the goal. Patrick tried to dive on the puck, but it was already too late—it had slipped in . . .

. . . just as it had slipped in when Lucky put Brian in goal. He'd told the rat to come out of the net every time to meet the puck when it came into their zone. Brian had done as he'd been told. What he hadn't been able to do was stop the puck when one of the Canadians skated past him and tipped it in.

Guido shook the memory out of his head, refusing to let the Canadians' lead get to him. Instead, he concentrated on slipping past a Canadian defenseman and bringing the puck into their zone. Gia followed him in on the other side of the ice. When there was an opening, he faked a shot and passed the puck. It was a beautiful pass, right to the center of her blade. Gia flicked her wrist, watching the puck sail into the lower right-hand corner of the net.

The crowd erupted.

Lucky immediately looked into the stands. Spike nodded. This was it. There were to be no more goals.

"All right, Gia!" Guido shouted. He raised his stick for her and tousled her helmet when she skated by.

Gia beamed, unable to hide her excitement.

Nerdy gave her a high-five.

"Nice job," said Marcello. "Our very own mon cherie gets us on the board!"

It was a great goal but no time to celebrate. It was the third period and there were only thirteen minutes left on the clock. If the Rink Rats wanted to win they had to seriously step up their game.

Lucky scrambled back and forth on the bench, nearly bending the clipboard in half. He knew this wasn't true; in order to win he had to stop sabotaging his team. Except . . . he couldn't do that. If he did, he and his sick mother would be out on the street. Not only that, but Spike would come after him. His stomach knotted at the thought—Spike made it a point that the rats he went after were never seen again.

A hand fell on Lucky's shoulder, nearly making him scream. He whirled around to find Angelo reaching up from his wheelchair.

"It looked like you needed some cheering up," he said.

Lucky could have told him he didn't know the half of it. "Thanks," he mumbled.

"Don't mention it. And try not to beat yourself up so much. The Canadians are a tough team. We all appreciate the hard work you've been putting in, coaching us."

That was a dagger to Lucky's heart. If only his team knew what he'd really been doing.

"We all believe in you," Angelo went on. "Your coaching has gotten us this far. There's still a chance. Just keep your head in the game."

Lucky looked back into the crowd. He knew what Spike

would do to him if he went back on the deal. But he also saw how much winning, not only this game but the championship, would mean to his team. This was most likely their last chance to win at home. After tonight, they might not have a home rink anymore.

Lucky squeezed his eyes closed, a million thoughts whirling around in his head. He stood like this for nearly a full minute before he opened them.

"You're right," he told Angelo, "there's still a chance."

Angelo clapped him on the back. "That's the spirit!"

"Time out!" Lucky shouted. He called the team over, pulling out a marker and furiously drawing a new play on the glass. He tapped on the *X*s and motioned to the arrows.

"Concentrate!" he told his team. "Don't get sloppy! We can take this back!"

The Rink Rats shouted approval. To them it felt like they had gotten their second wind. A new energy emanated from their coach, empowering them.

"For the championship!" Guido shouted.

"For the championship!" the team shouted back.

Chapter 24

Nerdy chased after the Canadian player. If the rat hadn't been twice his size, Nerdy's hit might have done something. As it was, Nerdy just bounced off, struggling to keep his balance.

The rat pulled his stick back and took a shot.

The puck whistled through the air and made a loud *Thwak!* when it struck the inside of Patrick's glove.

The crowd cheered.

Patrick wasted no time. He remembered the play his coach had just designed, and he slid the puck to Guido. Guido took the puck up, weaving in and out of the Canadians' defense.

He passed it to Gia, who passed it to Nerdy. Nerdy faked right and pulled it left before passing to Sergio. Sergio was already mid-slap shot when the puck came his way. His stick connected with it so hard that it sounded like a firecracker had gone off.

The horn that sounded was all the fans needed to hear. They rose out of their seats, screaming.

"Goal!" the referee shouted.

Spike glared at Lucky from the stands, his red eyes nearly fuming with hatred.

The referee shouted "goal!" three more times over the next eleven and a half minutes.

Now Spike's blazing gaze was hot enough to melt the ice. Lucky refused to look up. Instead he looked at the elated faces of his friends, hoping he'd made the right decision.

The crowd cheered as loud as they could, lending their strength and support. Nerdy knew they would need more than that alone to win. He desperately prayed for a miracle.

The last minute and a half on the clock ticked down, the score tied.

The puck dropped. Guido fought for it ferociously. One moment he had it, the next Pierre slapped it away.

Gia darted forward, intercepting it. She dropped her hip into the rat in front of her and passed it to Marcello. He faked right, then left, then left again. When the Canadian followed, he pushed right, bringing up the puck. He got maybe six or seven feet when a defenseman appeared.

Marcello passed.

Gia took the puck back, skating like the wind. She pushed it up the ice, Guido following close behind. Together they weaved in and out of the defensemen, interlacing an intricate pattern on the ice. If they had been in water they might have created a whirlpool.

The clock slipped past the one minute mark and began to tick down wildly. The seconds changed so fast it was hard to keep track.

"Hurry!" Lucky shouted. He gripped his clipboard so hard he would have marks on his paws later.

All the players on the bench watched, twisting the butts of their sticks and gnawing on their mouthpieces.

The Rink Rats fans in the crowd held their breath.

The Canadian fans shouted for defense.

Gia heard none of it. She was in the zone, only aware of the puck on her stick and the goalie in the net. He was watching her with intent ferocity. Each move she made, he tracked with his eyes. Even the subtlest of changes he was aware of. Gia knew they had no chance. Not when the Canadian goalie was in the zone.

That's why she did what she did next.

She passed the puck to Guido. As she did, she performed an elaborate twirl, her long blond hair streaming out of her helmet and spinning in a fan. Her plan worked. The goalie, unable to help himself, glanced in her direction. When he did, Guido closed his eyes and took the shot.

The puck parted the air, soaring towards the net. Everyone in the crowd held their breath, even the Canadian fans. Everybody just watched as it traveled towards the goal.

The Rink Rats closed their eyes, too, unable to watch.

The goalie pushed hard with his blade and shifted toward the side of the net. There was a loud, echoing *Ping!* and the puck struck the post.

The Rink Rats' hearts dropped. They knew what that sound implied. Each of them had hit the post on more than one occasion when taking practice shots. It was the sound of failure. Of getting so close to a goal but being denied by only a few inches.

Nerdy was the first to open his eyes. When he did, he stared, unbelieving. The puck was inside the net! It had hit the post, but it had bounced in directly after! Maybe it had ricocheted off the Canadian goalie. He didn't know, and he didn't care. All that mattered was that they had won! They had finally beaten the Canadians! And with only three seconds on the clock to spare!

For those next three seconds, it was impossible to hear anything in the rink. The referee dropped the puck, but it didn't matter—the Rink Rats fans were already celebrating, throwing their paws in the air and shouting. Angelo's grandmother sounded her bullhorn. Marcello's fan club stood up, dancing as their pink shirts spelled out his name.

The Rink Rats took it all in. When the buzzer sounded to officially end the game, they skated back to their bench and embraced each other in a humongous hug.

Gia threw off her helmet and wrapped her arms around Guido. "You were amazing out there!"

Guido felt his cheeks going red, but he didn't care. He knew it had to be now or never. "*You're* amazing," he said.

Now it was Gia's turn to blush. She didn't get to do it long because Guido leaned in and kissed her. She pulled away, blinking. When she was sure it had really happened, she leaned in and kissed him back.

Everyone around them cheered. Some because of their union, others because of the game.

"It's a miracle! It's a miracle!" Nerdy kept shouting. "We beat them! We won!"

"That was no miracle," Sergio said. "We trained hard and it paid off."

Nerdy cracked a smile. When Guido and Gia finally pulled apart, he gestured for Guido to look in his skate. Guido did, confused. What he found there made him smile as well. Tucked deep inside, nestled under the tongue of the skate, was a small thatch of the blessed straw. Guido pulled it out, holding it up.

It was true that training hard and practicing paid off, but a little extra luck never hurt any.

"Miracles," Guido said, laughing happily.

Lucky chanced a look in the stands, sure he'd see Spike glaring at him. Only . . . the rat was gone. Somehow his absence unsettled Lucky even more than his presence. It was enough to replace the pleasure he'd felt from winning with a sickening dread.

Chapter 25

The trophy was a big triple-decker piece of craftsmanship. A large black onyx pedestal supported the three engraved columns that held up the second onyx tier. Gold plating wound its way up these columns like twisting spires. At the very top of the third tier stood a gold rat dressed in hockey gear. It crouched down, bearing its teeth, its stick pulled back in a slap shot. At the bottom sat a reflective gold plate, engraved to spell out the words

LEAGUE CHAMPIONS

THE BROOKLYN RINK RATS

As the Rink Rats were celebrating, the referee skated over, handing them the trophy. There was no arguing. Everyone passed it to Guido, who they hoisted high over their heads, hooting and cheering. Everyone was in good spirits. Except for the Canadians. The Canadians and one other rat . . .

Chapter 26

Coach Lucky tumbled to the ground, snow filling his shirt and ice scratching his face. He tried to get to his feet but a boot shot out, kicking him in the side, sending him sprawling back to the ground.

"You were supposed to lose," said his attacker.

Lucky looked up. The blazing red eyes stood out in stark contrast against the cold winter sky.

"We had a deal," said Spike, "and you broke it."

His henchmen stepped in, kicking Lucky again, making sure he stayed on the ground. "What do you have to say for yourself?" Spike asked.

Lucky coughed, clutching his throbbing side. "I couldn't throw the game. My team practiced too hard. I never would have forgiven myself."

Spike shook his head, an expression of utter disappointment on his face. "Funny, you're never going to forgive yourself for winning either."

Each of the henchmen kicked him again. Lucky rolled over,

howling in pain. His insides felt like they were being tenderized.

"Stop!" he cried out. "Stop!"

Spike shook his head. "You should have thought about that before you double-crossed me."

"I'll pay you!" Lucky said desperately. "I'll pay you everything you lost."

"With what money?"

"I-I don't know. But I'll find some. I swear."

Spike shook his head. "I don't think so. Now's the time when you start paying for your actions." He glanced at his henchmen and snapped his fingers. "Marcus, Tyler, show this rat we mean business."

"You got it, boss," said Tyler. He was the smaller of the two, but it wouldn't have made the slightest of differences—they were each the size of two Canadian players easily. Considering the fact that the Canadians were big rats already, that made Spike's henchmen *huge!*

Tyler grabbed one of Lucky's wrists while Marcus grabbed the other. Together, they hoisted Lucky to his feet, holding his arms in the crooks of their elbows. They were so tall that Lucky barely touched the ground.

Spike walked up to him, surveying his prey. The cologne he wore was so cloying that Lucky could barely breathe.

"Please," he begged. "Give me a chance to make it up to

you."

"I already have, and you proved to me that you can't be trusted. It's such a shame I have to make you disappear. You would have been much more profitable if I could keep you around."

Lucky felt his heart skip. He understood what Spike meant by disappearing, and it scared him half to death.

He tried one last desperate attempt to save his life. "Isn't there anything I can do?"

Spike paused for a moment, genuinely considering the question. At last he said, "Yes, there is."

Lucky felt a rush of relief flood into his veins. "What is it? I'll do anything!"

Spike grinned maliciously. "You can make it easy."

Lucky did the complete opposite. Knowing all was lost, he squirmed, kicked, and fought to free himself. All his efforts were in vein. Spike's henchmen were so strong they barely even flinched.

"Help!" Lucky cried out, his voice echoing in the chill night air. "Somebody, please help me!"

Spike laughed. "Scream all you want, nobody's going to come."

Although that wasn't entirely true. A familiar figure lurked in the shadows, his tail curling, his nails digging furrows into the snow. He listened to the rats quarreling and licked his lips. He'd been denied a late-night snack twice already. He wasn't about to let that happen again.

For the entire confrontation, Lucky's eyes had been glued to Spike, unable to look away. Now, as the rat approached, they widened in terror, wandering off to something behind him.

Spike refused to look. He knew all the tricks in the book and wouldn't be fooled.

Only . . . the eyes of his henchmen were widening as well. They grew so big that Spike thought they might roll out of the rats' heads.

Finally, one of them opened their mouths. "Uh . . . boss . . ."

Spike turned around. By that time it was already too late. All that Spike saw before he was swept up into a hungry mouth were a pair of glaring yellow eyes.

"Run!" Marcus shouted. He dropped Lucky and took off down the alleyway. Tyler did the same thing at the same exact time. The two collided, sprawling to the snow. They shot up, rubbing their heads, and tried running again. That was when Sid the Alley Cat swatted them with his paw. They went tumbling, end over end, into the wall. Lucky didn't stick around. He had a nasty idea what would happen next and didn't want to watch. Instead, he scurried back to the rink, feeling as if he'd been given a second chance at life. This time he promised himself he wouldn't gamble it away.

Chapter 27

Christmas day arrived bright and sunny. The snow reflected the rays off its frozen surface and bounced them every which way, gleaming on homes, cars, and Christmas carolers. The latter went through the streets, filling Little Rataly with Christmas cheer.

Nerdy let their songs fill his ears as he ran through town. His grandmother had been absolutely right about the blessed straw. So far two of the miracles he wished for had come true. There was only one more left to go, and he desperately wanted to be there when it happened.

He stopped abruptly when he came to the pizzeria. The fire escape on the side of the building was down, and he scurried up the stairs.

"Guido, wake up!"

He pounded on the window as loud as he could.

In the room on the other side, Guido rolled over in his bed, pulling his covers up over his head.

"Guido!"

The blanket rustled as Guido tried to block out the sound. Nerdy kept pounding. Finally Guido threw the covers off.

"What is it?"

Nerdy didn't know whether to laugh or duck down and hide. In the end he decided on laughing. "I need you to wake up!"

Guido grunted, still half asleep. "I *am* up, thanks to you."

"Good, now follow me."

"Where?"

"To the Ice Palace!"

That took Guido by surprise. "The Ice Palace? Why?" Then a horrible thought occurred to him. "Was it all a dream? Please tell me we already beat the Canadians."

Nerdy had to stifle a giggle. "We beat them, all right. This is something else. There's one more miracle about to come true, and I need you to let me into the rink. I need to see it happen."

Under any other circumstances, Guido might have scuffed at the idea of miracles, but he had seen the blessed straw first-hand and just what it could do.

"Okay," he said. "I'll let you in. But only under one circumstance."

Nerdy thought that was fair. "What is it?"

Guido yawned, his mouth stretching so wide that he might have been able to fit a full apple in it. "You buy me a cup of coffee on the way."

. . .

The mood in the Ice Palace was nothing like the night before. Instead of the joyous cheers echoing throughout the arena, dismal sobs filled the office. They were so loud and rough that the hitching could be heard from halfway down the hall.

"Grandpa?" A.J. asked cautiously, stepping into the room.

Pops Anderson sat at his desk, his face buried in the crook of his arms, his thin chest trembling as he cried. When he heard A.J.'s voice, he quickly sat up, wiping away his tears with the back of his hand.

"Oh, A.J.," he said, sniffling. "I didn't hear you come in."

A.J. thought about asking his grandfather if he was okay, but he didn't want to embarrass the old man. Besides, he thought he knew the answer to his question anyway. Instead he said, "Today's the day Big Daddy takes back the rink, isn't it?"

Pops nodded glumly. "I'm afraid so. I just wish we could have saved it. Now your team won't have anywhere to practice."

"That's okay," said A.J. "The important thing is we have each other."

Pops couldn't help but smile. "You know, you're still so young, but sometimes I forget how mature you can be."

Now it was A.J.'s turn to smile. He looked around the office, taking it all in. "We had a good run."

"We did," Pops agreed. "What do you say I find my old skates and we go out on the ice one last time, just you and me?"

A.J. beamed. "That would be awesome!"

Hearing the genuine excitement in his grandson's voice was enough to raise his spirits. "Excellent. Just give me a few minutes to put them—"

He paused, his eyes fixing upon something.

"What?" A.J. asked.

Pops lifted the pen holder, picking up the thatch of blessed straw beneath. "What's this?"

A.J. studied it. "Looks like straw to me."

"It looks like straw to me, too. But what's straw doing here? And who could have gotten into my office without the ke—"

Before he could finish the question, a knock sounded at the door.

Both A.J. and Pops looked up. Then they looked at each other, wondering the same thing: *Did this have anything to do with the straw?* If Nerdy was in the conversation with them, he might have said that there was a pretty good chance it did.

The knock came again. This time A.J. opened the door. On the other side stood a man dressed in a black suit. His shoes were polished to such a degree that A.J. could see his face in them.

"Excuse me," said the man. "I'm looking for Anthony James Anderson Senior." He raised the leather briefcase in his hand. "I have some business to discuss with him."

Pops stood up, frustrated. "You can tell Big Daddy I'm not leaving until I skate one last time with my grandson."

The man looked confused. "You must have me mistaken for someone else. My name's James Mathers. I'm here representing the estate of your late son Anthony James Anderson Junior and his wife Maureen Anderson."

"That's my mom and dad," A.J. said.

Mr. Mathers nodded. "Indeed. May I come in?"

Pops gestured for him to have a seat. "Wait a minute, I don't understand. Why are we just meeting now?"

"Well," said Mr. Mathers, "I've been searching for you the past year in Minnesota, where your son lived, never realizing *you* lived in New York."

He crossed one leg over the other, put the briefcase on top, and opened it. From within, he pulled out a piece of paper, along with a check.

"It seems that James and Maureen had taken out a life insurance policy in case anything should happen to them. I'm here to make sure that money finds its way to its rightful beneficiary."

"A.J. . . . ." said Pops, looking at his grandson.

"I'm glad there's no confusion," said Mr. Mathers. "Again, my apologies that I could not find you sooner." He handed Pops the piece of paper. "Because you're A.J.'s legal guardian, I'll need you to sign this agreement stating that you're the recipient of the funds until he becomes of age."

Pops signed and took the check Mr. Mathers held out to him. He looked at the number written on it. His breath caught. His first thought was that he had read the number wrong—surely the decimal point was in a different place. His second thought was that this had to be a mistake. He was expecting around one hundred thousand dollars, maybe two at the most.

Mr. Mathers saw the look on his face. "I can assure you it's no mistake. Your son and daughter-in-law took out a very aggressive insurance policy."

Pops could barely speak. His throat felt as if somebody had poured a bucketful of sand down it.

"How much is it?" A.J. asked.

Instead of trying to speak, Pops handed A.J. the check.

A.J.'s eyes shot open. *"A million dollars!"*

"That's right, son," said Mr. Mathers. "Don't go spending it all in one place." He winked, but neither A.J. or his grandfather were paying attention. They were too busy staring at the check, their mouths agape.

"We can buy the rink from Big Daddy and fix it up," Pops said at last. He quickly turned to A.J. "That is, if you want to."

"Of course I do!" A.J. exclaimed. "It's a miracle!"

Smiling, Mr. Mathers sat back and laced his fingers together, taking in the scene before him. This was the best part of his job.

A.J. didn't let him sit for long. He sprang up and hugged the man, nearly toppling him over in the process. Pops got up, too, expressing his happiness the same way. The embrace lasted for a full minute. When they broke it, they could have sworn they heard cheerful squeaking coming from a hole in the wall.

Pops looked down at the blessed straw, still in his hand. He remembered the little rat scurrying across the office floor that one night and had an idea who might have left it for him.

"Thank you, my little friends," he said. "From the bottom of my heart, thank you."

Chapter 28

Tony's pizzeria sold the best pizza in Little Rataly. The dough was always cooked to perfection, and the cheese and sauce were paired up in just the right ratio to make the taste buds tingle. Perhaps this was why the Rink Rats chose the restaurant to host their celebration. Or maybe it had something to do with the fact that Guido had scored the winning goal and his parents owned it. Whatever the case, the Rink Rats found themselves in the back room seated around two long wooden tables that had been pushed together.

The room was decorated with green, white, and red streamers, along with balloons and a large banner that stretched from wall to wall, reading *CONGRATULATIONS!*

Every Rink Rat was in attendance, even Cream Puff (who was back from the hospital and sitting with Oscar the Kitten curled up comfortably on his lap) and Angelo, who balanced between a pair of crutches, the red cast still on his leg.

Guido's dad Tony brought out several pizzas, which the rats quickly cut up and shoved into their mouths. They had cheered for beating the Canadians and winning the championships, and they had cheered again when Guido and Nerdy told them the fantastic news about the rink being saved.

"Please tell me you're not joking," Sergio had said.

Nerdy had answered, "We're not. Guido and I were right there when this man came into Pops Anderson's office and gave him the money. Pops said he's buying the rink from that guy Big Daddy and fixing it up. It's gonna be nicer than ever!"

"That's great news," said Lucky.

"I'd say that's *fantastic* news," countered Brian.

"Yeah," agreed Patrick. "Now we don't have to go looking for another rink. We can finally call this one home."

"Home is definitely what it is," said Cream Puff. He scratched behind Oscar's ears. The kitten purred in delight, agreeing with him.

Marcello was equally in agreement. "Oui-oui, home is where the heart is."

"There's a lot of heart in that old rink," said Angelo. "Even for those just joining us."

Gia put her pizza down. "What do you mean by *just* joining? I've been at every game showing my support."

Guido took her paw in his. "I think he means just joining the team," he said with a playful smile.

"He better." She winked. "Or I may just have to check him into the boards at the next practice."

"Keep dreaming," said Angelo. "By then my knee will be better and you won't be able to catch me."

They went on, joking, laughing, filling the room with their merriment. Towards the end of the party, Cream Puff wheeled his chair over to Nerdy.

"I never got a chance to thank you," he said.

"For what?" asked Nerdy.

"For this . . ." He pulled some of the blessed straw out of his pocket and handed it to Nerdy. "I think it saved my life."

Nerdy took it, turning the straw over in his paw. "It's the least I could have done. When you're a Rink Rat, you're family."

"Well, in that case," said Cream Puff, "I have the best family in the world."

Nerdy hugged him. When Oscar meowed, he petted him, too. Towards the end of the evening, Nerdy excused himself, telling everyone he would be right back. He slipped out the back door and made his way down the street. When he came to the church at the corner, he stopped in front of the nativity scene.

He pulled the straw Cream Puff had given him out of his pocket. He stared at it for a long time. At last, he lifted up the baby Jesus and placed it back in the crib.

"Thank you, for the miracles," he said to nobody in particular.

At that moment, the wind picked up, lifting tiny flakes of snow that had accumulated on the nativity scene. They swirled around in the air, creating a magnificent display in the night sky before finally settling down. He wasn't sure if he heard a tiny whisper in that wind, but he liked to think he did, a whisper that said, *You're welcome.*

He stood there, thinking of how fortunate he and his friends were. Cream Puff had pulled through his coma, his team had finally beaten the Canadians, and the Ice Palace had been saved. That was a good thing, because they were all looking forward to the hockey season next year. Nerdy would surely be borrowing a little more of the blessed straw when the time came around. In fact, all the Rink Rats would. They did have a title to defend, after all.

THE TAIL END

Luciano "LUCKY" Grimaldi
Ht - 12 inches   *Weight - 2.80 lbs*
Games - 24   Goals - 15   Assts - 25   PIM - 30

Carmine "Cream Puff" Ponzini

Ht - 16 inches   **Weight - 7.55 lbs**

Games - 24   Goals - 10   Assts - 12   PIM - 10

Made in the USA
Middletown, DE
04 September 2019